'Munificent in its own mischievous, mortally serious way, *The Sea* by John Banville brought new tidings of this arch-stylist's gifts, and won timely recognition of them'

Seamus Heaney, Books of the Year, *TLS*

'Poetry seems to come easily to Banville, a writer at the top of his game . . . There is so much to applaud in this book that it deserves more than one reading. The prose aside, John Banville is a great structural craftsman. Nothing is rushed, nothing thrown away, no incident stretched beyond what it is worth'　　　Chris Paling, *Literary Review*

'[Banville] is prodigiously gifted. He cannot write an unpolished phrase, so we read him slowly, relishing the stream of pleasures he affords. Everything in Banville's books is alive. Bleakly elegant, he is a writer's writer, a new Henry Green, who can conjure the poetry of people and places. He relishes language, and wants it to work for him anew. So he uses virtuoso coinages . . . everything interests him'　　　Peter J. Conradi, *Independent*

'In *The Sea* Banville has written an utterly absorbing novel about the strange workings of grief, and the gratuitous dramas of memory . . . No one since Proust has been better able to recover the charged and dreamy atmospheres of what seems to be childhood'

Adam Phillips, *London Review of Books*

'With his fastidious wit and exquisite style, John Banville is the heir to Nabokov. *The Sea* [is] his best novel so far . . . Banville's prose is sublime' ***Daily Telegraph***

'Banville writes novels of complex patterning, with grace, precision and timing, and there are wonderful digressive meditations . . . This is a writer who is not indifferent to the world's indifference' ***Guardian***

'In *The Sea*, as in all Banville's best work, the linguistic inventiveness is at the service of a haunting emotion'

Prospect

'A beautiful novel, challenging and richly rewarding . . . It is a comfort to know that we have a lord of language among us' ***Irish Independent***

'*The Sea* is an excellent choice, reaffirming the Man Booker as a prize of some distinction' ***Herald***

'As much a philosopher as a novelist, Banville's achievement has been to explore the strangeness and dislocation of existence . . . His uncompromising bravery remains, even more so than the Booker win, a cause for celebration'

Sunday Times

The Sea

JOHN BANVILLE was born in
Wexford, Ireland, in 1945. He is the author
of fifteen novels including *The Sea*, which won
the 2005 Man Booker Prize. He has received a
literary award from the Lannan Foundation.
He lives in Dublin.

ALSO BY JOHN BANVILLE

Long Lankin

Nightspawn

Birchwood

Doctor Copernicus

Kepler

The Newton Letter

Mefisto

The Book of Evidence

Ghosts

Athena

The Untouchable

Eclipse

Shroud

The Infinities

JOHN BANVILLE

The Sea

PICADOR

First published 2005 by Picador

First published in paperback 2005 by Picador

This edition published 2006 by Picador
an imprint of Pan Macmillan
20 New Wharf Road, London N1 9RR
Associated companies throughout the world
www.panmacmillan.com

ISBN 978-0-330-48329-2

A CIP catalogue record for this book is available from
the British Library.

Typeset by Intype London Ltd
Printed and bound by CPI Group (UK) Ltd, Croydon, CR0 4YY

Visit www.picador.com to read more about all our books
and to buy them. You will also find features, author interviews and
news of any author events, and you can sign up for e-newsletters
so that you're always first to hear about our new releases.

To Colm, Douglas, Ellen, Alice

I

THEY DEPARTED, the gods, on the day of the strange tide. All morning under a milky sky the waters in the bay had swelled and swelled, rising to unheard-of heights, the small waves creeping over parched sand that for years had known no wetting save for rain and lapping the very bases of the dunes. The rusted hulk of the freighter that had run aground at the far end of the bay longer ago than any of us could remember must have thought it was being granted a relaunch. I would not swim again, after that day. The seabirds mewled and swooped, unnerved, it seemed, by the spectacle of that vast bowl of water bulging like a blister, lead-blue and malignantly agleam. They looked unnaturally white, that day, those birds. The waves were depositing a fringe of soiled yellow foam along the waterline. No sail marred the high horizon. I would not swim, no, not ever again.

Someone has just walked over my grave. Someone.

The name of the house is the Cedars, as of old. A bristling clump of those trees, monkey-brown with a tarry reek, their trunks nightmarishly tangled, still grows at the left side, facing across an untidy lawn to the big curved window of what used to be the living room but which Miss Vavasour prefers to call, in landladyese, the lounge. The front door is at the opposite side, opening on to a square of oil-stained gravel behind the iron gate that is still painted green, though rust has reduced its struts to a tremulous filigree. I am amazed at how little has changed in the more than fifty years that have gone by since I was last here. Amazed, and disappointed, I would go so far as to say appalled, for reasons that are obscure to me, since why should I desire change, I who have come back to live amidst the rubble of the past? I wonder why the house was built like that, sideways-on, turning a pebble-dashed windowless white end-wall to the road; perhaps in former times, before the railway, the road ran in a different orientation altogether, passing directly in front of the front door, anything is possible. Miss V. is vague on dates but thinks a cottage was first put up here early in the last century, I mean the century before last, I am losing track of the millennia, and then was added on to haphazardly over the years. That would account for the jumbled look of the place, with small rooms giving on to bigger ones, and windows facing blank walls, and low ceilings throughout. The pitchpine floors sound a nautical note, as does my spindle-backed swivel chair. I imagine an old seafarer dozing by the fire, landlubbered at last, and the winter gale rattling the window frames. Oh, to be him. To have been him.

When I was here all those years ago, in the time of the gods, the Cedars was a summer house, for rent by the fortnight or the month. During all of June each year a rich doctor and his large, raucous family infested it – we did not like the doctor's loud-voiced children, they laughed at us and threw stones from behind the unbreachable barrier of the gate – and after them a mysterious middle-aged couple came, who spoke to no one, and grimly walked their sausage dog in silence at the same time every morning down Station Road to the strand. August was the most interesting month at the Cedars, for us. The tenants then were different each year, people from England or the Continent, the odd pair of honeymooners whom we would try to spy on, and once even a fit-up troupe of itinerant theatre people who were putting on an afternoon show in the village's galvanised-tin cinema. And then, that year, came the family Grace.

The first thing I saw of them was their motor car, parked on the gravel inside the gate. It was a low-slung, scarred and battered black model with beige leather seats and a big spoked polished wood steering wheel. Books with bleached and dog-eared covers were thrown carelessly on the shelf under the sportily raked back window, and there was a touring map of France, much used. The front door of the house stood wide open, and I could hear voices inside, downstairs, and from upstairs the sound of bare feet running on floorboards and a girl laughing. I had paused by the gate, frankly eavesdropping, and now suddenly a man with a drink in his hand came out of the house. He was short and top-heavy, all shoulders and chest and big round head, with close-cut, crinkled, glittering-black hair with flecks of premature grey in it and a pointed black beard likewise flecked. He wore a loose green shirt unbuttoned and khaki shorts and was barefoot. His skin was so deeply tanned by the sun it had a purplish sheen. Even his feet, I noticed, were brown on the insteps; the majority of fathers in my experience were fish-belly white below the collar-line. He set his tumbler – ice-blue gin and ice cubes and a lemon slice – at a perilous angle on the roof of the car and opened the passenger door and leaned inside to rummage for something under the dashboard. In the unseen upstairs of the house the girl laughed again and gave a wild, warbling cry of mock-panic, and again there was the sound of scampering feet. They were playing chase, she and the voiceless other. The man straightened and took his glass of gin from the roof and slammed the car door. Whatever it was he had been searching for he had not found. As he turned back to the house his eye caught mine and he winked. He did not do it in the way that adults usually did, at once arch and ingratiating. No, this was a comradely, a conspiratorial wink, masonic, almost, as if this moment that we, two strangers, adult and boy, had shared, although outwardly without significance, without content, even, nevertheless had meaning. His eyes were an extraordinary pale transparent shade of blue. He went back inside then, already talking before he was through the door. 'Damned thing,' he said, 'seems to be . . .' and was gone. I lingered a moment, scanning the upstairs windows. No face appeared there.

That, then, was my first encounter with the Graces: the girl's voice coming down from on high, the running footsteps, and the man here below with the blue eyes giving me that wink, jaunty, intimate and faintly satanic.

Just now I caught myself at it again, that thin, wintry whistling through the front teeth that I have begun to do recently. *Deedle deedle deedle*, it goes, like a dentist's drill. My father used to whistle like that, am I turning into him? In the room across the corridor Colonel Blunden is playing the wireless. He favours the afternoon talk programmes, the ones in which irate members of the public call up to complain about villainous politicians and the price of drink and other perennial irritants. 'Company,' he says shortly, and clears his throat, looking a little abashed, his protuberant, parboiled eyes avoiding mine, even though I have issued no challenge. Does he lie on the bed while he listens? Hard to picture him there in his thick grey woollen socks, twiddling his toes, his tie off and shirt collar agape and hands clasped behind that stringy old neck of his. Out of his room he is vertical man itself, from the soles of his much-mended glossy brown brogues to the tip of his conical skull. He has his hair cut every Saturday morning by the village barber, short-back-and-sides, no quarter given, only a hawkish stiff grey crest left on top. His long-lobed leathery ears stick out, they look as if they had been dried and smoked; the whites of his eyes too have a smoky yellow tinge. I can hear the buzz of voices on his wireless but cannot make out what they say. I may go mad here. *Deedle deedle.*

Later that day, the day the Graces came, or the following one, or the one following that, I saw the black car again, recognised it at once as it went bounding over the little humpbacked bridge that spanned the railway line. It is still there, that bridge, just beyond the station. Yes, things endure, while the living lapse. The car was heading out of the village in the direction of the town, I shall call it Ballymore, a dozen miles away. The town is Ballymore, this village is Ballyless, ridiculously, perhaps, but I do not care. The man with the beard who had winked at me was at the wheel, saying something and laughing, his head thrown back. Beside him a woman sat with an elbow out of the rolled-down window, her head back too, pale hair shaking in the gusts from the window, but she was not laughing only smiling, that smile she reserved for him, sceptical, tolerant, languidly amused. She wore a white blouse and sunglasses with white plastic rims and was smoking a cigarette. Where am I, lurking in what place of vantage? I do not see myself. They were gone in a moment, the car's sashaying back-end scooting around a bend in the road with a spurt of exhaust smoke. Tall grasses in the ditch, blond like the woman's hair, shivered briefly and returned to their former dreaming stillness.

I walked down Station Road in the sunlit emptiness of afternoon. The beach at the foot of the hill was a fawn shimmer under indigo. At the seaside all is narrow horizontals, the world reduced to a few long straight lines pressed between earth and sky. I approached the Cedars circumspectly. How is it that in childhood everything new that caught my interest had an aura of the uncanny, since according to all the authorities the uncanny is not some new thing but a thing known returning in a different form, become a revenant? So many unanswerables, this the least of them. As I approached I heard a regular rusty screeching sound. A boy of my age was draped on the green gate, his arms hanging limply down from the top bar, propelling himself with one foot slowly back and forth in a quarter circle over the gravel. He had the same straw-pale hair as the woman in the car and the man's unmistakable azure eyes. As I walked slowly past, and indeed I may even have paused, or faltered, rather, he stuck the toe of his plimsoll into the gravel to stop the swinging gate and looked at me with an expression of hostile enquiry. It was the way we all looked at each other, we children, on first encounter. Behind him I could see all the way down the narrow garden at the back of the house to the diagonal row of trees skirting the railway line – they are gone now, those trees, cut down to make way for a row of pastel-coloured bungalows like dolls' houses – and beyond, even, inland, to where the fields rose and there were cows, and tiny bright bursts of yellow that were gorse bushes, and a solitary distant spire, and then the sky, with scrolled white clouds. Suddenly, startlingly, the boy pulled a grotesque face at me, crossing his eyes and letting his tongue loll on his lower lip. I walked on, conscious of his mocking eye following me.

Plimsoll. Now, there is a word one does not hear any more, or rarely, very rarely. Originally sailors' footwear, from someone's name, if I recall, and something to do with ships. The Colonel is off to the lavatory again. Prostate trouble, I bet. Going past my door he softens his tread, creaking on tiptoe, out of respect for the bereaved. A stickler for the observances, our gallant Colonel.

I am walking down Station Road.

So much of life was stillness then, when we were young, or so it seems now; a biding stillness; a vigilance. We were waiting in our as yet unfashioned world, scanning the future as the boy and I had scanned each other, like soldiers in the field, watching for what was to come. At the bottom of the hill I stopped and stood and looked three ways, along Strand Road, and back up Station Road, and the other way, towards the tin cinema and the public tennis courts. No one. The road beyond the tennis courts was called the Cliff Walk, although whatever cliffs there may once have been the sea had long ago eroded. It was said there was a church submerged in the sandy sea bed down there, intact, with bell tower and bell, that once had stood on a headland that was gone too, brought toppling into the roiling waves one immemorial night of tempest and awful flood. Those were the stories the locals told, such as Duignan the dairyman and deaf Colfer who earned his living selling salvaged golf balls, to make us transients think their tame little seaside village had been of old a place of terrors. The sign over the Strand Café, advertising cigarettes, Navy Cut, with a picture of a bearded sailor inside a lifebuoy, or a ring of rope – was it? – creaked in the sea breeze on its salt-rusted hinges, an echo of the gate at the Cedars on which for all I knew the boy was swinging yet. They creak, this present gate, that past sign, to this day, to this night, in my dreams. I set off along Strand Road. Houses, shops, two hotels – the Golf, the Beach – a granite church, Myler's grocery-cum-post-office-cum-pub, and then the field – the Field – of wooden chalets one of which was our holiday home, my father's, my mother's, and mine.

If the people in the car were his parents had they left the boy on his own in the house? And where was the girl, the girl who had laughed?

The past beats inside me like a second heart.

The consultant's name was Mr Todd. This can only be considered a joke in bad taste on the part of polyglot fate. It could have been worse. There is a name De'Ath, with that fancy medial capital and apotropaic apostrophe which fool no one. This Todd addressed Anna as Mrs Morden but called me Max. I was not at all sure I liked the distinction thus made, or the gruff familiarity of his tone. His office, no, his rooms, one says rooms, as one calls him Mister not

Doctor, seemed at first sight an eyrie, although they were only on the third floor. The building was a new one, all glass and steel – there was even a glass-and-steel tubular lift shaft, aptly suggestive of the barrel of a syringe, through which the lift rose and fell hummingly like a giant plunger being alternately pulled and pressed – and two walls of his main consulting room were sheets of plate glass from floor to ceiling. When Anna and I were shown in my eyes were dazzled by a blaze of early-autumn sunlight falling down through those vast panes. The receptionist, a blonde blur in a nurse's coat and sensible shoes that squeaked – on such an occasion who would really notice the receptionist? – laid Anna's file on Mr Todd's desk and squeakingly withdrew. Mr Todd bade us sit. I could not tolerate the thought of settling myself on a chair and went instead and stood at the glass wall, looking out. Directly below me there was an oak, or perhaps it was a beech, I am never sure of those big deciduous trees, certainly not an elm since they are all dead, but a noble thing, anyway, the summer's green of its broad canopy hardly silvered yet with autumn's hoar. Car roofs glared. A young woman in a dark suit was walking away swiftly across the car park, even at that distance I fancied I could hear her high heels tinnily clicking on the tarmac.

Anna was palely reflected in the glass before me, sitting very straight on the metal chair in three-quarters profile, being the model patient, with one knee crossed on the other and her joined hands resting on her thigh. Mr Todd sat sideways at his desk riffling through the documents in her file; the pale-pink cardboard of the folder made me think of those shivery first mornings back at school after the summer holidays, the feel of brand-new schoolbooks and the somehow bodeful smell of ink and pared pencils. How the mind wanders, even on the most concentrated of occasions.

I turned from the glass, the outside become intolerable now.

Mr Todd was a burly man, not tall or heavy but very broad: one had an impression of squareness. He cultivated a reassuringly old-fashioned manner. He wore a tweed suit with a waistcoat and watch chain, and chestnut-brown brogues that Colonel Blunden would have approved. His hair was oiled in the style of an earlier time, brushed back sternly from his forehead, and he had a moustache, short and bristly, that gave him a dogged look. I realised with a mild shock that despite these calculatedly venerable effects he could not be much more than fifty. Since when did doctors start being younger than I am? On he wrote, playing for time; I did not blame him, I would have done the same, in his place. At last he put down his pen but still was disinclined to speak, giving the earnest impression of not knowing where to begin or how. There was something studied about this hesitancy, something theatrical. Again, I understand. A doctor must be as good an actor as physician. Anna shifted on her chair impatiently.

'Well, Doctor,' she said, a little too loudly, putting on the bright, tough tone of one of those film stars of the Forties, 'is it the death sentence, or do I get life?'

The room was still. Her sally of wit, surely rehearsed, had fallen flat. I had an urge to rush forward and snatch her up in my arms, fireman-fashion, and carry her bodily out of there. I did not stir. Mr Todd looked at her in mild, hare-eyed panic, his eyebrows hovering halfway up his forehead.

'Oh, we won't let you go quite yet, Mrs Morden,' he said, showing big grey teeth in an awful smile. 'No, indeed we will not.'

Another beat of silence followed that. Anna's hands were in her lap, she looked at them, frowning, as if she had not noticed them before. My right knee took fright and set to twitching.

Mr Todd launched into a forceful disquisition, polished from repeated use, on promising treatments, new drugs, the mighty arsenal of chemical weapons he had at his command; he might have been speaking of magic potions, the alchemist's physic. Anna continued frowning at her hands; she was not listening. At last he stopped and sat gazing at her with the same desperate, leporine look as before, audibly breathing, his lips drawn back in a sort of leer and those teeth on show again.

'Thank you,' she said politely in a voice that seemed now to come from very far off. She nodded to herself. 'Yes,' more remotely still, 'thank you.'

At that, as if released, Mr Todd gave his knees a quick smack with two flat palms and jumped to his feet and fairly bustled us to the door. When Anna had gone through he turned to me and gave me a gritty, man-to-man smile, and the handshake, dry, brisk, unflinching, which I am sure he reserves for the spouses at moments such as this.

The carpeted corridor absorbed our footsteps.

The lift, pressed, plunged.

We walked out into the day as if we were stepping on to a new planet, one where no one lived but us.

*

17

Arrived home, we sat outside the house in the car for a long time, loath of venturing in upon the known, saying nothing, strangers to ourselves and each other as we suddenly were. Anna looked out across the bay where the furled yachts bristled in the glistening sunlight. Her belly was swollen, a round hard lump pressing against the waistband of her skirt. She had said people would think she was pregnant – 'At my age!' – and we had laughed, not looking at each other. The gulls that nested in our chimneys had all gone back to sea by now, or migrated, or whatever it is they do. Throughout that drear summer they had wheeled above the rooftops all day long, jeering at our attempts to pretend that all was well, nothing amiss, the world continuous. But there it was, squatting in her lap, the bulge that was big baby De'Ath, burgeoning inside her, biding its time.

At last we went inside, having nowhere else to go. Bright light of midday streamed in at the kitchen window and everything had a glassy, hard-edged radiance as if I were scanning the room through a camera lens. There was an impression of general, tight-lipped awkwardness, of all these homely things – jars on the shelves, saucepans on the stove, that breadboard with its jagged knife – averting their gaze from our all at once unfamiliar, afflicted presence in their midst. This, I realised miserably, this is how it would be from now on, wherever she goes the soundless clapping of the leper's bell preceding her. *How well you look!* they would exclaim, *Why, we've never seen you better!* And she with her brilliant smile, putting on a brave face, poor Mrs Bones.

She stood in the middle of the floor in her coat and scarf, hands on her hips, casting about her with a vexed expression. She was still handsome then, high of cheekbone, her skin translucent, paper-fine. I always admired in particular her Attic profile, the nose a line of carven ivory falling sheer from the brow.

'Do you know what it is?' she said with bitter vehemence. 'It's inappropriate, that's what it is.'

I looked aside quickly for fear my eyes would give me away; one's eyes are always those of someone else, the mad and desperate dwarf crouched within. I knew what she meant. This was not supposed to have befallen her. It was not supposed to have befallen us, we were not that kind of people. Misfortune, illness, untimely death, these things happen to good folk, the humble ones, the salt of the earth, not to Anna, not to me. In the midst of the imperial progress that was our life together a grinning losel had stepped out of the cheering crowd and sketching a parody of a bow had handed my tragic queen the warrant of impeachment.

She put on a kettle of water to boil and fished in a pocket of her coat and brought out her spectacles and put them on, looping the string behind her neck. She began to weep, absent-mindedly, it might be, making no sound. I moved clumsily to embrace her but she drew back sharply.

'For heaven's sake don't fuss!' she snapped. 'I'm only dying, after all.'

The kettle came to the boil and switched itself off and the seething water inside it settled down grumpily. I marvelled, not for the first time, at the cruel complacency of ordinary things. But no, not cruel, not complacent, only indifferent, as how could they be otherwise? Henceforth I would have to address things as they are, not as I might imagine them, for this was a new version of reality. I took up the teapot and the tea, making them rattle – my hands were shaking – but she said no, she had changed her mind, it was brandy she wanted, brandy, and a cigarette, she who did not smoke, and rarely drank. She gave me the dull glare of a defiant child, standing there by the table in her coat. Her tears had stopped. She took off her glasses and dropped them to hang below her throat on their string and rubbed at her eyes with the heels of her hands. I found the brandy bottle and tremblingly poured a measure into a tumbler, the bottle-neck and the rim of the glass chattering against each other like teeth. There were no cigarettes in the house, where was I to get cigarettes? She said it was no matter, she did not really want to smoke. The steel kettle shone, a slow furl of steam at its spout, vaguely suggestive of genie and lamp. Oh, grant me a wish, just the one.

'Take off your coat, at least,' I said.

But why at least? What a business it is, the human discourse.

I gave her the glass of brandy and she stood holding it but did not drink. Light from the window behind me shone on the lenses of her spectacles where they hung at her collar bone, giving the eerie effect of another, miniature she standing close in front of her under her chin with eyes cast down. Abruptly she went slack and sat down heavily, extending her arms before her along the table in a strange, desperate-seeming gesture, as if in supplication to some unseen other seated opposite her in judgment. The tumbler in her hand knocked on the wood and splashed out half its contents. Helplessly I contemplated her. For a giddy second the notion seized me that I would never again be able to think of another word to say to her, that we would go on like this, in agonised inarticulacy, to the end. I bent and kissed the pale patch on the crown of her head the size of a sixpence where her dark hair whorled. She turned her face up to me briefly with a black look.

'You smell of hospitals,' she said. 'That should be me.'

I took the tumbler from her hand and put it to my lips and drank at a draught what remained of the scorching brandy. I realised what the feeling was that had been besetting me since I had stepped that morning into the glassy glare of Mr Todd's consulting rooms. It was embarrassment. Anna felt it as well, I was sure of it. Embarrassment, yes, a panic-stricken sense of not knowing what to say, where to look, how to behave, and something else, too, that was not quite anger but a sort of surly annoyance, a surly resentment at the predicament in which we grimly found ourselves. It was as if a secret had been imparted to us so dirty, so nasty, that we could hardly bear to remain in one another's company yet were unable to break free, each knowing the foul thing that the other knew and bound together by that very knowledge. From this day forward all would be dissembling. There would be no other way to live with death.

Still Anna sat erect there at the table, facing away from me, her arms extended and hands lying inert with palms upturned as if for something to be dropped into them.

'Well?' she said without turning. 'What now?'

There goes the Colonel, creeping back to his room. That was a long session in the lav. Strangury, nice word. Mine is the one bedroom in the house which is, as Miss Vavasour puts it with a demure little moue, *en suite*. Also I have a view, or would have were it not for those blasted bungalows at the bottom of the garden. My bed is daunting, a stately, high-built, Italianate affair fit for a Doge, the headboard scrolled and polished like a Stradivarius. I must enquire of Miss V. as to its provenance. This would have been the master bedroom when the Graces were here. In those days I never got further than the downstairs, except in my dreams.

I have just noticed today's date. It is a year exactly since that first visit Anna and I were forced to pay to Mr Todd in his rooms. What a coincidence. Or not, perhaps; are there coincidences in Pluto's realm, amidst the trackless wastes of which I wander lost, a lyreless Orpheus? Twelve months, though! I should have kept a diary. My journal of the plague year.

A dream it was that drew me here. In it, I was walking along a country road, that was all. It was in winter, at dusk, or else it was a strange sort of dimly radiant night, the sort of night that there is only in dreams, and a wet snow was falling. I was determinedly on my way somewhere, going home, it seemed, although I did not know what or where exactly home might be. There was open land to my right, flat and undistinguished with not a house or hovel in sight, and to my left a deep line of darkly louring trees bordering the road. The branches were not bare despite the season, and the thick, almost black leaves drooped in masses, laden with snow that had turned to soft, translucent ice. Something had broken down, a car, no, a bicycle, a boy's bicycle, for as well as being the age I am now I was a boy as well, a big awkward boy, yes, and on my way home, it must have been home, or somewhere that had been home, once, and that I would recognise again, when I got there. I had hours of walking to do but I did not mind that, for this was a journey of surpassing but inexplicable importance, one that I must make and was bound to complete. I was calm in myself, quite calm, and confident, too, despite not knowing rightly where I was going except that I was going home. I was alone on the road. The snow which had been slowly drifting down all day was unmarked by tracks of any kind, tyre, boot or hoof, for no one had passed this way and no one would. There was something the matter with my foot, the left one, I must have injured it, but long ago, for it was not painful, though at every step I had to throw it out awkwardly in a sort of half-circle, and this hindered me, not seriously but seriously enough. I felt compassion for myself, that is to say the dreamer that I was felt compassion for the self being dreamed, this poor lummox going along dauntlessly in the snow at fall of day with only the road ahead of him and no promise of homecoming.

That was all there was in the dream. The journey did not end, I arrived nowhere, and nothing happened. I was just walking there, bereft and stalwart, endlessly trudging through the snow and the wintry gloaming. But I woke into the murk of dawn not as I usually do these days, with the sense of having been flayed of yet another layer of protective skin during the night, but with the conviction that something had been achieved, or at least initiated. Immediately then, and for the first time in I do not know how long, I thought of Ballyless and the house there on Station Road, and the Graces, and Chloe Grace, I cannot think why, and it was as if I had stepped suddenly out of the dark into a splash of pale, salt-washed sunlight. It endured only a minute, less than a minute, that happy lightsomeness, but it told me what to do, and where I must go.

I first saw her, Chloe Grace, on the beach. It was a bright, wind-worried day and the Graces were settled in a shallow recess scooped into the dunes by wind and tides to which their somewhat raffish presence lent a suggestion of the proscenium. They were impressively equipped, with a faded length of striped canvas strung between poles to keep chill breezes off, and folding chairs and a little folding table, and a straw hamper as big as a small suitcase containing bottles and vacuum flasks and tins of sandwiches and biscuits; they even had real tea cups, with saucers. This was a part of the beach that was tacitly reserved for residents of the Golf Hotel, the lawn of which ended just behind the dunes, and indignant stares were being directed at these heedlessly interloping villa people with their smart beach furniture and their bottles of wine, stares which the Graces if they noticed them ignored. Mr Grace, Carlo Grace, Daddy, was wearing shorts again, and a candy-striped blazer over a chest that was bare save for two big tufts of tight curls in the shape of a miniature pair of widespread fuzzy wings. I had never before encountered nor, I think, have I encountered since, anyone so fascinatingly hairy. On his head was clamped a canvas hat like a child's upturned sand bucket. He was sitting on one of the folding chairs, holding a newspaper open before him and at the same time managing to smoke a cigarette, despite the stiff wafts of wind coming in from the sea. The blond boy, the swinger on the gate – it was Myles, I may as well give him his name – was crouched at his father's feet, pouting moodily and delving in the sand with a jagged piece of sea-polished driftwood. Some way behind them, in the shelter of the dune wall, a girl, or young woman, was kneeling on the sand, wrapped in a big red towel, under the cover of which she was trying vexedly to wriggle herself free of what would turn out to be a wet bathing suit. She was markedly pale and soulful of expression, with a long, slender face and very black, heavy hair. I noticed that she kept glancing, resentfully, as it seemed, at the back of

Carlo Grace's head. I noticed too that the boy Myles was keeping sidelong watch, in the evident hope, which I shared, that the girl's protective towel would slip. She could hardly be his sister, then.

Mrs Grace came up the beach. She had been in the sea and was wearing a black swimsuit, tight and darkly lustrous as sealskin, and over it a sort of wraparound skirt made of some diaphanous stuff, held at the waist with a single button and billowing open with each step she took to reveal her bare, tanned, rather thick but shapely legs. She stopped in front of her husband and pushed her white-rimmed sunglasses up into her hair and waited through the beat that he allowed to pass before he lowered the newspaper and looked up at her, lifting his hand that held the cigarette and shading his eyes against the salt-sharpened light. She said something and he put his head on one side and shrugged, and smiled, showing numerous small white even teeth. Behind him the girl, still under the towel, discarded her bathing suit that she had freed herself of at last and, turning her back, sat down on the sand with her legs flexed and made the towel into a tent around herself and rested her forehead on her knees, and Myles drove his stick into the sand with disappointed force.

So there they were, the Graces: Carlo Grace and his wife Constance, their son Myles, the girl or young woman who I was sure was not the girl I had heard laughing in the house that first day, with all their things around them, their folding chairs and tea cups and tumblers of white wine, and Connie Grace's revealing skirt and her husband's funny hat and newspaper and cigarette, and Myles's stick, and the girl's swimsuit, lying where she had tossed it, limply wadded and stuck along one wet edge with a fringe of sand, like something thrown up drowned out of the sea.

I do not know for how long Chloe had been standing on the dune before she jumped. She may have been there all that time, watching me watching the others. She was first a silhouette, with the sun behind her making a shining helmet of her short-cropped hair. Then she lifted her arms and with her knees pressed together launched herself off the dune wall. The air made the legs of her shorts balloon briefly. She was barefoot, and landed on her heels, sending up a shower of sand. The girl under the towel – Rose, give her a name too, poor Rosie – uttered a little shriek of fright. Chloe wobbled, her arms still lifted and her heels in the sand, and it seemed she would fall over or at least sit down hard, but instead she kept her balance, and smiled sideways spitefully at Rose who had sand in her eyes and was making a fish face and shaking her head and blinking. '*Chlo*-e!' Mrs Grace said, a reproving wail, but Chloe ignored her and came forward and knelt in the sand beside her brother and tried to wrest the stick from him. I was lying on my stomach on a towel with my cheeks propped on my hands, pretending to read a book. Chloe knew I was looking at her and seemed not to care. What age were we, ten, eleven? Say eleven, it will do. Her chest was as flat as Myles's, her hips were no wider than mine. She wore a white singlet over her shorts. Her sun-bleached hair was almost white. Myles, who had been battling to keep his stick, snatched it free of her grasp at last and hit her with it on the knuckles and she said 'Ow!' and struck him in the breastbone with a small, pointed fist.

'Listen to this advertisement,' her father said to no one in particular, and read aloud, laughing, from the newspaper. '*Live ferrets required as venetian blind salesmen. Must be car drivers. Apply box twenty-three.*' He laughed again, and coughed, and, coughing, laughed. 'Live ferrets!' he cried. 'Oh, my.'

How flat all sounds are at the seaside, flat and yet emphatic, like the sound of gunshots heard at a distance. It must be the muffling effect of so much sand. Although I cannot say when I have had occasion to hear a gun or guns being fired.

Mrs Grace poured wine for herself, tasted it, grimaced, and sat down in a folding chair and crossed one firm leg on the other, her beach shoe dangling. Rose was getting dressed fumblingly under her towel. Now it was Chloe's turn to draw her knees up to her chest – is it a thing all girls do, or did, at least, sitting that way in the shape of a zed fallen over on its front? – and hold her feet in her hands. Myles poked her in the side with his stick. 'Daddy,' she said with listless irritation, 'tell him to stop.' Her father went on reading. Connie Grace's dangling shoe was jiggling in time to some rhythm in her head. The sand around me with the sun strong on it gave off its mysterious, catty smell. Out on the bay a white sail shivered and flipped to leeward and for a second the world tilted. Someone away down the beach was calling to someone else. Children. Bathers. A wire-haired ginger dog. The sail turned to windward again and I heard distinctly from across the water the ruffle and snap of the canvas. Then the breeze dropped and for a moment all went still.

They played a game, Chloe and Myles and Mrs Grace, the children lobbing a ball to each other over their mother's head and she running and leaping to try to catch it, mostly in vain. When she runs her skirt billows behind her and I cannot take my eyes off the tight black bulge at the upside-down apex of her lap. She jumps, grasping air and giving breathless cries and laughing. Her breasts bounce. The sight of her is almost alarming. A creature with so many mounds and scoops of flesh to carry should not cavort like this, she will damage something inside her, some tender arrangement of adipose tissue and pearly cartilage. Her husband has lowered his newspaper and is watching her too, combing his fingers through his beard under his chin and coldly smiling, his lips drawn back a little from those fine small teeth and his nostrils flared wolfishly as if he is trying to catch her scent. His look is one of arousal, amusement and faint contempt; he seems to want to see her fall down in the sand and hurt herself; I imagine hitting him, punching him in the exact centre of his hairy chest as Chloe had punched her brother. Already I know these people, am one of them. And I have fallen in love with Mrs Grace.

Rose comes out of the towel, in red shirt and black slacks, like a magician's assistant appearing from under the magician's scarlet-lined cape, and busies herself in not looking at anything, especially the woman and her children at play.

Abruptly Chloe loses interest in the game and turns aside and flops down in the sand. How well I will come to know these sudden shifts of mood of hers, these sudden sulks. Her mother calls to her to come back and play but she does not respond. She is lying propped on an elbow on her side with her ankles crossed, looking past me narrow-eyed out to sea. Myles does a chimp dance in front of her, flapping his hands under his armpits and gibbering. She pretends to be able to see through him. 'Brat,' her mother says of her spoilsport daughter, almost complacently, and goes back and sits down on her chair. She is out of breath, and the smooth, sand-coloured slope of her bosom heaves. She lifts a hand up high to brush a clinging strand of hair from her damp forehead and I fix on the secret shadow under her armpit, plum-blue, the tint of my humid fantasies for nights to come. Chloe sulks. Myles goes back to delving violently in the sand with his stick. Their father folds his newspaper and squints at the sky. Rose is examining a loose button on her shirt. The little waves rise and plash, the ginger dog barks. And my life is changed forever.

But then, at what moment, of all our moments,

is life not utterly, utterly changed, until the final, most momentous change of all?

We holidayed here every summer, my father and mother and I. We would not have put it that way. *We came here for our holidays*, that is what we would have said. How difficult now it is to speak as I spoke then. We came for our holidays here every summer, for many years, many years, until my father ran off to England, as fathers sometimes did, in those days, and do still, for that matter. The chalet that we rented was a slightly less than life-sized wooden model of a house. It had three rooms, a living room at the front that was also a kitchen and two tiny bedrooms at the back. There were no ceilings, only the sloped undersides of the tarpapered roof. The walls were panelled with unintentionally elegant, narrow, bevelled boards that on sunny days smelled of paint and pine-sap. My mother cooked on a paraffin stove, the tiny fuel-hole of which afforded me an obscurely furtive pleasure when I was called on to clean it, employing for the task a delicate instrument made of a strip of pliant tin with a stiff filament of wire protruding at a right angle from its tip. I wonder where it is now, that little Primus stove, so sturdy and steadfast? There was no electricity and at night we lived by the light of an oil lamp. My father worked in Ballymore and came down in the evenings on the train, in a wordless fury, bearing the frustrations of his day like so much luggage clutched in his clenched fists. What did my mother do with her time when he was gone and I was not there? I picture her sitting at the oilcloth-covered table in that little wooden house, a hand under her head, nursing her disaffections as the long day wanes. She was still young then, they both were, my father and my mother, younger certainly than I am now. How strange a thing that is to think of. Everybody seems to be younger than I am, even the dead. I see them there, my poor parents, rancorously playing at house in the childhood of the world. Their unhappiness was one of the constants of my earliest years, a high, unceasing buzz just beyond hearing. I did not hate them. I loved them, probably. Only they were in my way, obscuring my view of the future. In time I would be able to see right through them, my transparent parents.

My mother would only bathe far up the beach, away from the eyes of the hotel crowds and the noisy encampments of day trippers. Up there, past where the golf course began, there was a permanent sandbank a little way out from shore that enclosed a shallow lagoon when the tide was right. In those soupy waters she would wallow with small, mistrustful pleasure, not swimming, for she could not swim, but stretched out full-length on the surface and walking along the sea-floor on her hands, straining to keep her mouth above the lapping wavelets. She wore a crimplene swimsuit, mouse-pink, with a coy little hem stretched across tight just below the crotch. Her face looked bare and defenceless, pinched in the tight rubber seal of her bathing cap. My father was a fair swimmer, going at a sort of hindered, horizontal scramble with mechanical strokes and a gasping sideways grimace and one starting eye. At the end of a length he would rise up, panting and spitting, his hair plastered down and ears sticking out and black trunks abulge, and stand with hands on hips and watch my mother's clumsy efforts with a faint, sardonic grin, a muscle in his jaw twitching. He splashed water in her face and seized her wrists and wading backwards hauled her through the water. She shut her eyes tight and shrieked at him furiously to stop. I watched these edgy larks in a paroxysm of disgust. At last he let her go and turned on me, upending me and grasping me by the ankles and pushing me forward wheelbarrow-fashion off the edge of the sandbank and laughing. How strong his hands were, like manacles of cold, pliant iron, I feel even yet their violent grip. He was a violent man, a man of violent gestures, violent jokes, but timid, too, no wonder he left us, had to leave us. I swallowed water, and twisted out of his grasp in a panic and jumped to my feet and stood in the surf, retching.

Chloe Grace and her brother were standing on the hard sand at the water's edge, looking on.

They wore shorts as usual and were barefoot. I saw how strikingly alike they were. They had been collecting seashells, which Chloe was carrying in a handkerchief knotted corner-to-corner to make a pouch. They stood regarding us without expression, as if we were a show, a comic turn that had been laid on for them but which they found not very interesting, or funny, but peculiar only. I am sure I blushed, grey and goosepimpled though I was, and I had an acute awareness of the thin stream of seawater pouring in an unstoppable arc out of the sagging front of my swimming-trunks. Had it been in my power I would have cancelled my shaming parents on the spot, would have popped them like bubbles of sea spray, my fat little bare-faced mother and my father whose body might have been made of lard. A breeze smacked down on the beach and swarmed across it slantwise under a skim of dry sand, then came on over the water, chopping the surface into sharp little metallic shards. I shivered, not from the cold now but as if something had passed through me, silent, swift, irresistible. The pair on the shore turned and trailed off in the direction of the wrecked freighter.

Was it that day that I noticed Myles's toes were webbed?

Miss Vavasour downstairs is playing the piano. She maintains a delicate touch on the keys, trying not to be heard. She worries that she will disturb me, engaged as I am up here in my immense and unimaginably important labours. She plays Chopin very nicely. I hope she does not start on John Field, I could not bear that. Early on I tried to interest her in Fauré, the late nocturnes in particular, which I greatly admire. I even bought the scores for her, ordered them from London, at considerable expense. I was too ambitious. She says she cannot get her fingers around the notes. *Your mind*, more like, I do not reply. Recreant, recreant thoughts. I wonder that she never married. She was beautiful, once, in her soulful way. Nowadays she wears her long grey hair, that formerly was so black, gathered into a tight loop behind her head and transpierced by two crossed pins as big as knitting needles, a style that is to my mind suggestive, wholly inappropriately, of the geisha-house. The Japanese note is continued in the kimono-like belted silk dressing-gown that she wears of a morning, the silk printed with a motif of brightly coloured birds and bamboo fronds. At other times of the day she favours sensible tweeds, but at dinner-time she may surprise us, the Colonel and me, coming rustling to the table in a calf-length confection of lime-green with a sash, or in Spanish-style scarlet bolero jacket and tapered black slacks and neat little shiny black slippers. She is quite the elegant old lady, and registers with a muted flutter my approving glance.

The Cedars has retained hardly anything of the past, of the part of the past that I knew here. I had hoped for something definite of the Graces, no matter how small or seemingly insignificant, a faded photo, say, forgotten in a drawer, a lock of hair, or even a hair-pin, lodged between the floorboards, but there was nothing, nothing like that. No remembered atmosphere, either, to speak of. I suppose so many of the living passing through — it is a lodging house, after all — have worn away all traces of the dead.

How wildly the wind blows today, thumping its

big soft ineffectual fists on the window panes. This is just the kind of autumn weather, tempestuous and clear, that I have always loved. I find the autumn stimulating, as spring is supposed to be for others. Autumn is the time to work, I am at one with Pushkin on that. Oh, yes, Alexandr and I, Octobrists both. A general costiveness has set in, however, most unPushkinian, and I cannot work. But I keep to my table, pushing the paragraphs about like the counters in a game I no longer know how to play. The table is a small spindly affair with an undependable flap, which Miss V. carried up here herself and presented to me with a certain shy intentionality. *Creak, little wood thing, creak.* There is my sea-captain's swivel chair too, just like the one I used to have in some rented place where we lived years ago, Anna and I, it even groans in the same way when I lean back in it. The work I am supposed to be engaged in is a monograph on Bonnard, a modest project in which I have been mired for more years than I care to compute. A very great painter, in my estimation, about whom, as I long ago came to realise, I have nothing of any originality to say. Brides-in-the-Bath, Anna used to call him, with a cackle. *Bonnard, Bonn'art, Bon'nargue.* No, I cannot work, only doodle like this.

Anyway, work is not the word I would apply to what I do. Work is too large a term, too serious. Workers work. The great ones work. As for us middling men, there is no word sufficiently modest that yet will be adequate to describe what we do and how we do it. Dabble I do not accept. It is amateurs who dabble, while we, the class or genus of which I speak, are nothing if not professional. Wallpaper manufacturers such as Vuillard and Maurice Denis were every bit as diligent – there is another key word – as their friend Bonnard, but diligence is not, is never, enough. We are not skivers, we are not lazy. In fact, we are frenetically energetic, in spasms, but we are free, fatally free, of what might be called the curse of perpetuance. We finish things, while for the real worker, as the poet Valéry, I believe it was, pronounced, there is no finishing a work, only the abandoning of it. A nice vignette has Bonnard at the Musée du Luxembourg with a friend, it was Vuillard, indeed, if I am not mistaken, whom he sets to distracting the museum guard while he whips out his paint-box and reworks a patch of a picture of his own that had been hanging there for years. The true workers all die in a fidget of frustration. So much to do, and so much left undone!

Ouch. There is that pricking sensation again. I

cannot help wondering if it might presage something serious. Anna's first signs were of the subtlest. I have become quite the expert in matters medical this past year, not surprisingly. For instance I know that pins-and-needles in the extremities is one of the early symptoms of multiple sclerosis. This sensation I have is like pins-and-needles only more so. It is a burning jab, or series of jabs, in my arm, or in the back of my neck, or once, even, memorably, on the upper side of the knuckle of my right big toe, which sent me hopping on one leg about the room uttering piteous moos of distress. The pain, or smart, though brief, is often severe. It is as if I were being tested for vital signs; for signs of feeling; for signs of life.

Anna used to laugh at me for my hypochondriacal ways. *Doctor Max*, she would call me. *How is Doctor Max today, is he feeling poorly?* She was right, of course, I have always been a moaner, fussing over every slightest twinge or ache.

There is that robin, it flies down from somewhere every afternoon and perches on the holly bush beside the garden shed. I notice it favours doing things by threes, hopping from a top twig to a lower and then a lower again where it stops and whistles thrice its sharp, assertive note. All creatures have their habits. Now from the other side of the garden a neighbour's piebald cat comes creeping, soft-stepping pard. Watch out, birdie. That grass needs cutting, once more will suffice, for this year. I should offer to do it. The thought occurs and at once there I am, in shirt-sleeves and concertina trousers, stumbling sweat-stained behind the mower, grass-haulms in my mouth and the flies buzzing about my head. Odd, how often I see myself like this these days, at a distance, being someone else and doing things that only someone else would do. Mow the lawn, indeed. The shed, although tumbledown, is really rather handsome when looked at with a sympathetic eye, the wood of it weathered to a silky, silvery grey, like the handle of a well-worn implement, a spade, say, or a trusty axe. Old Brides-in-the-Bath would have caught that texture exactly, the quiet sheen and shimmer of it. *Doodle deedle dee.*

Claire, my daughter, has written to ask how I am faring. Not well, I regret to say, bright Clarinda, not well at all. She does not telephone because I have warned her I will take no calls, even from her. Not that there are any calls, since I told no one save her where I was going. What age is she now, twenty-something, I am not sure. She is very bright, quite the bluestocking. Not beautiful, however, I admitted that to myself long ago. I cannot pretend this is not a disappointment, for I had hoped that she would be another Anna. She is too tall and stark, her rusty hair is coarse and untameable and stands out around her freckled face in an unbecoming manner, and when she smiles she shows her upper gums, glistening and whitely pink. With those spindly legs and big bum, that hair, the long neck especially – that is something at least she has of her mother – she always makes me think, shamefacedly, of Tenniel's drawing of Alice when she has taken a nibble from the magic mushroom. Yet she is brave and makes the best of herself and of the world. She has the rueful, grimly humorous, clomping way to her that is common to so many ungainly girls. If she were to arrive here now she would come sweeping in and plump herself down on my sofa and thrust her clasped hands so far down between her knees the knuckles would almost touch the floor, and purse her lips and inflate her cheeks and say *Poh!* and launch into a litany of the comic mishaps she has suffered since last we saw each other. Dear Claire, my sweet girl.

She accompanied me when I came down here to Ballyless for the first time, after that dream, the dream I had of walking homeward in the snow. I think she was worried I might be bent on drowning myself. She must not know what a coward I am. The journey down reminded me a little of the old days, for she and I were always fond of a jaunt. When she was a child and could not sleep at night – from the start she was an insomniac, just like her Daddy – I would bundle her in a blanket into the car and drive her along the coast road for miles beside the darkling sea, crooning whatever songs I knew any of the words of, which far from putting her to sleep made her clap her hands in not altogether derisory delight and cry for more. One time, later on, we even went on a motoring holiday together, just the two of us, but it was a mistake, she was an adolescent by then and grew rapidly bored with vineyards and chateaux and my company, and nagged at me stridently without let-up until I gave in and brought her home early. The trip down here turned out to be not much better.

It was a sumptuous, oh, truly a sumptuous autumn day, all Byzantine coppers and golds under a Tiepolo sky of enamelled blue, the countryside all fixed and glassy, seeming not so much itself as its own reflection in the still surface of a lake. It was the kind of day on which, latterly, the sun for me is the world's fat eye looking on in rich enjoyment as I writhe in my misery. Claire was wearing a big coat of dun-coloured suede which in the warmth of the car gave off a faint but unmistakable fleshy stink which distressed me, although I made no complaint. I have always suffered from what I think must be an overly acute awareness of the mingled aromas that emanate from the human concourse. Or perhaps suffer is the wrong word. I like, for instance, the brownish odour of women's hair when it is in need of washing. My daughter, a fastidious spinster – alas, I am convinced she will never marry – usually has no smell at all, that I can detect. That is another of the numerous ways in which she differs from her mother, whose feral reek, for me the stewy fragrance of life itself, and which the strongest perfume could not quite suppress, was the thing that first drew me to her, all those years ago. My hands now, eerily, have a trace of the same smell, her smell, I cannot rid them of it, wring them though I may. In her last months she smelt, at her best, of the pharmacopoeia.

When we arrived I marvelled to see how much of the village as I remembered it was still here, if only for eyes that knew where to look, mine, that is. It was like encountering an old flame behind whose features thickened by age the slender lineaments that

46

a former self so loved can still be clearly discerned. We passed the deserted railway station and came bowling over the little bridge – still intact, still in place! – my stomach at the crest doing that remembered sudden upward float and fall, and there it all was before me, the hill road, and the beach at the bottom, and the sea. I did not stop at the house but only slowed as we went by. There are moments when the past has a force so strong it seems one might be annihilated by it.

'That was it!' I said to Claire excitedly. 'The Cedars!' On the way down I had told her all, or almost all, about the Graces. 'That was where they stayed.'

She turned back in her seat to look.

'Why did you not stop?' she said.

What was I to answer? That I was overcome by a crippling shyness suddenly, here in the midst of the lost world? I drove on, and turned on to Strand Road. The Strand Café was gone, its place taken by a large, squat and remarkably ugly house. Here were the two hotels, smaller and shabbier, of course, than in my memory of them, the Golf sporting importantly a rather grandiose flag on its roof. Even from inside the car we could hear the palms on the lawn in front dreamily clacking their dry fronds, a sound

47

that on purple summer nights long ago had seemed to promise all of Araby. Now under the bronzen sunlight of the October afternoon – the shadows were lengthening already – everything had a quaintly faded look, as if it were all a series of pictures from old postcards. Myler's pub-post-office-grocery had swelled into a gaudy superstore with a paved parking area in front. I recalled how on a deserted, silent, sun-dazed afternoon half a century ago there had sidled up to me on the gravelled patch outside Myler's a small and harmless-seeming dog which when I put out my hand to it bared its teeth in what I mistakenly took to be an ingratiating grin and bit me on the wrist with an astonishingly swift snap of its jaws and then ran off, sniggering, or so it seemed to me; and how when I came home my mother scolded me bitterly for my foolishness in offering my hand to the brute and sent me, all on my own, to the village doctor who, elegant and urbane, stuck a perfunctory plaster over the rather pretty, purplish swelling on my wrist and then bade me take off all my clothes and sit on his knee so that, with a wonderfully pale, plump and surely manicured hand pressed warmly against my lower abdomen, he might demonstrate to me the proper way to breathe. 'Let the stomach swell instead of drawing it in, you see?'

he said softly, purringly, the warmth of his big bland face beating against my ear.

Claire gave a colourless laugh. 'Which left the more lasting mark,' she asked, 'the dog's teeth or the doctor's paw?'

I showed her my wrist where in the skin over the ulnar styloid are still to be seen the faint remaining scars from the pair of puncture marks made there by the canine's canines.

'It was not Capri,' I said, 'and Doctor ffrench was not Tiberius.'

In truth I have only fond memories of that day. I can still recall the aroma of after-lunch coffee on the doctor's breath and the fishy swivel of his house-keeper's eye as she saw me to the front door.

Claire and I arrived at the Field.

In fact it is a field no longer but a dreary holiday estate packed higgledy-piggledy with what are bound to be jerrybuilt bungalows, designed I suspect by the same cackhanded line-drawer who was responsible for the eyesores at the bottom of the garden here. However, I was pleased to note that the name given to the place, ersatz though it be, is The Lupins, and that the builder, for I presume it was the builder, even spared a tall stand of this modest wild shrub – *Lupinus*, a genus of the Papilionaceae, I have just looked it up – beside the ridiculously grand mock-gothic gateway that leads in from the road. It was under the lupin bushes that my father every other week, at darkest midnight, with spade and flashlight, muttering curses under his breath, would dig a hole in the soft sandy earth and bury the bucketful of slops from our chemical lavatory. I can never smell the weak but oddly anthropic perfume of those blossoms without seeming to catch behind it a lingering sweet whiff of nightsoil.

'Are you not going to stop at all?' Claire said. 'I'm starting to feel car-sick.'

As the years go on I have the illusion that my daughter is catching up on me in age and that by now we are almost contemporaries. It is probably the consequence of having such a clever child – had she persisted she would have made a far finer scholar than I could ever have hoped to be. Also she understands me to a degree that is disturbing and will not indulge my foibles and excesses as others do who know me less and therefore fear me more. But I am bereaved and wounded and require indulging. If there is a long version of shrift then that is what I am in need of. *Let me alone*, I cried at her in my mind, *let me creep past the traduced old Cedars, past the vanished Strand Café, past the Lupins and the Field that was, past all this past, for if I stop I shall surely dissolve in a shaming puddle of tears.* Meekly, however, I halted the car at the side of the road and she got out in a vexed silence and slammed the door behind her as if she were delivering me a box on the ear. What had I done to annoy her so? There are times when she is as wilfully moody as her mother.

And then suddenly, unlikeliest of all, behind the huddle of the Lupins' leprechaun houses, here was Duignan's lane, rutted as it always was, ambling between tangled hedges of hawthorn and dusted-over brambles. How had it survived the depredations of lorry and crane, of diggers both mechanical and human? Here as a boy I would walk down every morning, barefoot and bearing a dented billycan, on my way to buy the day's milk from Duignan the dairyman or his stoically cheerful, big-hipped wife. Even though the sun would be long up the night's moist coolness would cling on in the cobbled yard, where hens picked their way with finical steps among their own chalk-and-olive-green droppings. There was always a dog lying tethered under a leaning cart that would eye me measuringly as I went past, teetering on tiptoe so as to keep my heels out of the chicken-merd, and a grimy white cart-horse that would come and put its head over the half-door of the barn and regard me sidelong with an amused and sceptical eye from under a forelock that was exactly the same smoky shade of creamy-white as honeysuckle blossom. I did not like to knock at the farmhouse door, fearing Duignan's mother, a low-sized squarish old party who seemed fitted with a stumpy leg at each corner and who gasped when she breathed and lolled the pale wet polyp of her tongue on her lower lip, and instead I would hang back in the violet shadow of the barn to wait for Duignan or his missus to appear and save me from an encounter with the crone.

Duignan was a gangling pinhead with thin sandy hair and invisible eyelashes. He wore collarless calico shirts that were antique even then and shapeless trousers shoved into mud-caked wellingtons. In the dairy as he ladled out the milk he would talk to me about girls in a suggestively hoarse, wispy voice – he was to die presently of a diseased throat – saying he was sure I must have a little girlfriend of my own and wanting to know if she let me kiss her. As he spoke he kept his eye fixed on the long thin flute of milk he was pouring into my can, smiling to himself and rapidly batting those colourless lashes. Creepy though he was he held a certain fascination for me. He seemed always teasingly on the point of revealing, as he might show a lewd picture, some large, general and disgusting piece of knowledge to which only adults were privy. The dairy was a low square white-washed cell so white it was almost blue. The steel milk churns looked like squat sentries in flat hats, and each one had an identical white rosette burning on its shoulder where the light from the doorway was reflected. Big shallow muslin-draped pans of milk lost in their own silence were set on the floor to separate, and there was a hand-cranked wooden butter churn that I always wanted to see being operated but never did. The cool thick secret smell of milk made me think of Mrs Grace, and I would have a darkly exciting urge to give in to Duignan's wheedling and tell him about her, but held back, wisely, no doubt.

Now here I was at the farm gate again, the child of those days grown corpulent and half-grey and almost old. An ill-painted sign on the gate-post warned trespassers of prosecution. Claire behind me was saying something about farmers and shotguns but I paid no heed. I advanced across the cobbles – there were still cobbles! – seeming not to walk but bounce, rather, awkward as a half-inflated barrage balloon, buffeted by successive breath-robbing blows out of the past. Here was the barn and its half-door. A rusted harrow leaned where Duignan's cart used to lean – was the cart a misremembrance? The dairy was there too, but disused, its crazy door padlocked, against whom, it was impossible to imagine, the window panes dirtied over or broken and grass growing on the roof. An elaborate porch had been built on to the front of the farmhouse, a glass and aluminium gazebo of a thing suggestive of the rudimentary eye of a giant insect. Now inside it the door opened and an elderly young woman appeared and stopped behind the glass and considered me warily. I blundered forward, grinning and nodding, like a big bumbling missionary approaching the tiny queen of some happily as yet unconverted pygmy tribe. At first she stayed cautiously inside the porch while I addressed her through the glass, loudly enunciating my name and making excited gesticulations with my hands. Still she stood and gazed. She gave the impression of a young actress elaborately but not quite convincingly made up to look old. Her hair, dyed the colour of brown boot polish and permed into a mass of tight, shiny waves, was too voluminous for her little pinched face, surrounding it like a halo of dense thorns, and looking more like a wig than real hair. She wore a faded apron over a jumper that she could only have knitted herself, a man's corduroy trousers balding at the knees, and those zippered ankle boots of Prussian-blue mock-velvet that were all the rage among old ladies when I was young and latterly seem exclusive to beggar women and female winos. I bellowed at her through the glass how I used to stay down here as a child, in a chalet in the Field, and how I would come to the farm in the mornings for milk. She listened, nodding, a pucker appearing and disappearing at the side of her mouth as if she were suppressing a laugh. At last she opened the door of the porch and stepped out on to the cobbles. In my mood of half-demented euphoria – really, I was ridiculously excited – I had an urge to embrace her. I spoke in a rush of the Duignans, man and wife, of Duignan's mother, of the dairy, even of the baleful dog. Still she nodded, a seemingly disbelieving eyebrow arched, and looked past me to where Claire stood waiting in the gateway, arms folded, clasping herself in her big expensive fur-trimmed coat.

Avril, the young woman said her name was. Avril. She did not volunteer a surname. Dimly, like something lifting itself up that for a long time had seemed dead, there came to me the memory of a child in a dirty smock hanging back in the flagged hallway of the farmhouse, holding negligently by its chubby flexed arm a pink, bald and naked doll and watching me with a gnomic stare that nothing would deflect.

But this person before me could not have been that child, who by now would be, what, in her fifties? Perhaps the remembered child was a sister of this one, but much older, that is, born much earlier? Could that be? No, Duignan had died young, in his forties, so it was not possible, surely, that this Avril would be his daughter, since he was an adult when I was a child and . . . My mind balked in its calculations like a confused and weary old beast of burden. But Avril, now. Who in these parts would have conferred on their child a name so delicately vernal?

I asked again about the Duignans and Avril said yes, Christy Duignan had died – Christy? had I known that Duignan's name was Christy? – but Mrs D. was living still, in a nursing home somewhere along the coast. 'And Patsy has a place over near Old Bawn and Mary is in England but poor Willie died.' I nodded. I found it suddenly dispiriting to hear of them, these offshoots of the Duignan dynasty, so solid even in only their names, so mundanely real, Patsy the farmer and Mary the emigrant and little Willie who died, all crowding in on my private ceremony of remembering like uninvited poor relations at a fancy funeral. I could think of nothing to say. All the levitant euphoria of a moment past was gone now and I felt over-fleshed and incommensurate with the moment, standing there smiling and weakly nodding, the last of the air leaking out of me. Still Avril had not identified herself beyond the name, and seemed to think that I must know her, must have recognised her – but how would I, or from where, even though she was standing in what was once the Duignans' doorway? I wondered that she knew so much about the Duignans if she was not one of them, as it seemed certain she was not, or not of the immediate family, anyway, all those Willies and Marys and Patsys, none of whom could have been her parent or doubtless she would have said so by now. All at once my gloom gathered itself into a surge of sour resentment against her, as if she had for some fell reason of her own set herself up here, in this unconvincing disguise – that hennaed hair, those old lady's bootees – intentionally to usurp a corner of my mythic past. The greyish skin of her face, I noticed, was sprinkled all over with tiny freckles. They were not russet-coloured like Claire's, nor like the big splashy ones that used to swarm on Christy Duignan's strangely girlish forearms, nor, for that matter, like the worrying ones that nowadays have begun to appear on the backs of my own hands and on the chicken-pale flesh in the declivities of my shoulders on either side of the clavicle notch, but were much darker, of the same shade of dull brown as Claire's coat, hardly bigger than pinpricks and, I regret to say, suggestive of a chronic and general lack of cleanliness. They put me uneasily in mind of something, yet I could not think what it was.

'It is just, you see,' I said, 'that my wife died.'

I do not know what came over me to blurt it out like that. I hoped Claire behind me had not heard. Avril gazed into my face without expression, expecting me to say more, no doubt. But what more could I have said? On some announcements there is no elaborating. She gave a shrug denoting sympathy, lifting one shoulder and her mouth at one side.

'That's a pity,' she said in a plain, flat tone. 'I'm sorry to hear that.' She did not seem to mean it, somehow.

The autumn sun fell slantwise into the yard, making the cobbles bluely shine, and in the porch a pot of geraniums flourished aloft their last burning blossoms of the season. Honestly, this world.

In the flocculent hush of the Golf Hotel we seemed, my daughter and I, to be the only patrons. Claire wanted afternoon tea and when I had ordered it we were directed to a deserted cold conservatory at the rear that looked out on the strand and the receding tide. Here despite the glacial air a muted hint of past carousings lingered. There was a mingled smell of spilt beer and stale cigarette smoke, and on a dais in a corner an upright piano stood, incongruously bespeaking the Wild West, its lid lifted, showing the gapped grimace of its keys. After that encounter in the farmyard I felt quivery and vapourish, like a diva tottering offstage at the end of a disastrous night of broken high notes, missed prompts, collapsing scenery. Claire and I sat down side by side on a sofa and presently an awkward, ginger-haired boy tricked out in a waiter's black jacket and trousers with a stripe down the sides brought a tray and set it clattering on a low table before us and fled, stumbling in his big shoes. The tea-bag is a vile invention, suggestive to my perhaps overly squeamish eye of something a careless person might leave behind unflushed in the lavatory. I poured a cup of the turf-coloured tea and bolstered it with a nip from my hip-flask – never to be without a ready supply of anaesthetic, that is a thing I have learned in this past year. The light of afternoon was soiled and wintry now and a wall of cloud, dense, mud-blue, was building up from the horizon. The waves clawed at the suave sand along the waterline, scrabbling to hold

59

their ground but steadily failing. There were more palm trees out there, tousled and spindly, their grey bark looking thick and tough as elephant hide. A hardy breed they must be, to survive in this cold northern clime. Do their cells remember the desert's furnace-heat? My daughter sat sunk in her coat with both hands wrapped for warmth around her tea cup. I noted with a pang her babyish fingernails, their pale-lilac tint. One's child is always one's child.

I talked about the Field, the chalet, the Duignans.

'You live in the past,' she said.

I was about to give a sharp reply, but paused. She was right, after all. Life, authentic life, is supposed to be all struggle, unflagging action and affirmation, the will butting its blunt head against the world's wall, suchlike, but when I look back I see that the greater part of my energies was always given over to the simple search for shelter, for comfort, for, yes, I admit, it, for cosiness. This is a surprising, not to say a shocking, realisation. Before, I saw myself as something of a buccaneer, facing all-comers with a cutlass in my teeth, but now I am compelled to acknowledge that this was a delusion. To be concealed, protected, guarded, that is all I have ever truly wanted, to burrow down into a place of womby warmth and cower there, hidden from the sky's indifferent gaze and the harsh air's damagings. That is why the past is just such a retreat for me, I go there eagerly, rubbing my hands and shaking off the cold present and the colder future. And yet, what existence, really, does it have, the past? After all, it is only what the present was, once, the present that is gone, no more than that. And yet.

Claire drew her head tortoise-fashion deep into the shell of her coat and kicked off her shoes and braced her feet against the edge of the little table. There is always something touching in the sight of a woman's stockinged feet, I think it must be the way the toes are bunched fatly together so that they might almost be fused. Myles Grace's toes were naturally, unnaturally, like that. When he splayed them, which he could do as easily as if they were fingers, the membranes between them would stretch into a gossamer webbing, pink and translucent and shot through leaf-like with a tracery of fine veins red like covered flame, the marks of a godling, sure as heaven.

I suddenly recalled, out of the evening's steadily densening blue, the family of teddy bears that had been Claire's companions throughout her childhood. Slightly repulsive, animate-seeming things I thought them. Leaning over her in the grainy light of the bedside lamp to bid her goodnight I would find myself regarded from above the rim of her coverlet by half a dozen pairs of tiny gleaming glass eyes, wetly brown, motionless, uncannily alert.

'Your *lares familiares*,' I said now. 'I suppose you have them still, propped on your maiden couch?'

A steep-slanted flash of sunlight fell along the beach, turning the sand above the waterline bone-white, and a white seabird, dazzling against the wall of cloud, flew up on sickle wings and turned with a soundless snap and plunged itself, a shutting chevron, into the sea's unruly back. Claire sat motionless for a moment and then began to cry. No sound, only the tears, bright beads of quicksilver in the last effulgence of marine light falling down from the high wall of glass in front of us. Crying, in that silent and almost incidental fashion, is another thing she does just like her mother did.

'You're not the only one who is suffering,' she said.

I know so little about her, really, my daughter. One day when she was young, twelve or thirteen, I suppose, and poised on the threshold of puberty, I barged in on her in the bathroom, the door of which she had neglected to lock. She was naked save for a towel wrapped tightly turban-fashion around her head. She turned to look at me over her shoulder in a fall of calm light from the frosted window, quite unflustered, gazing at me out of the fulness of herself. Her breasts were still buds but already she had that big melony behind. What did I feel, seeing her there? An inner chaos, overlaid by tenderness and a kind of fright. Ten years later she abandoned her studies in art history – Vaublin and the fête galante style; that's my girl, or was – to take up the teaching of backward children in one of the city's increasingly numerous, seething slums. What a waste of talent. I could not forgive her, cannot still. I try, but fail. It was all the doing of a young man, a bookish fellow of scant chin and extreme egalitarian views, on whom she had set her heart. The affair, if such it was – I suspect she is still a virgin – ended badly for her. Having persuaded her to throw up what should have been her life's work in favour of a futile social gesture, the black-guard absconded, leaving my misfortunate girl in the lurch. I wanted to go after him and kill him. At the least, I said, let me pay for a good barrister to prosecute him for breach of promise. Anna said to stop it, that I was only making matters worse. She was already ill. What could I do?

Outside, the dusk was thickening. The sea that before had been silent had now set up a vague tumult, perhaps the tide was on the turn. Claire's tears had stopped but stood unwiped, she seemed not to have noticed them. I shivered; these days whole church-yardsful of mourners traipse back and forth unfeelingly over my grave.

A large man in a morning coat came from the doorway behind us and advanced soundlessly on servant's feet and looked at us in polite enquiry and met my eye and went away again. Claire snuffled, and delving in a pocket brought out a handkerchief and stentorously blew her nose.

'It depends,' I said mildly, 'on what you mean by suffering.'

She said nothing but put the hankie away and stood up and looked about her, frowningly, as if in search of something but not knowing what. She said she would wait for me in the car, and walked away with her head bowed and her hands deep in the pockets of that coat-shaped pelt. I sighed. Against a blackening vault of sky the seabirds rose and dived like torn scraps of rag. I realised I had a headache, it had been beating away unheeded in my skull since I had first sat down in this glassed-in box of wearied air.

The boy-waiter came back, tentative as a fox cub, and made to take the tray, a carroty lock falling limply forward from his brow. With that colouring he could be yet another of the Duignan clan, cadet branch. I asked him his name. He stopped, canted forward awkwardly from the waist, and looked at me from under his pale brows in speculative alarm. His jacket had a shine, the shot cuffs of his shirt were soiled.

'Billy, sir,' he said.

I gave him a coin and he thanked me and stowed it and took up the tray and turned, then hesitated.

'Are you all right, sir?' he said.

I brought out the car keys and looked at them in perplexity. Everything seemed to be something else. I said that yes, I was all right, and he went away. The silence about me was heavy as the sea. The piano on the dais grinned its ghastly grin.

When I was leaving the lobby the man in the morning coat was there. He had a large, waxen, curiously characterless face. He bowed to me, beaming, hands clasped into fists before his chest in an excessive, operatic gesture. What is it about such people that makes me remember them? His look was unctuous yet in some way minatory. Perhaps I had been expected to tip him also. As I say: this world.

Claire was waiting by the car, shoulders hunched, using the sleeves of her coat for a muff.

'You should have asked me for the key,' I said. 'Did you think I wouldn't give it to you?'

On the way home she insisted on taking the wheel, despite my vigorous resistance. It was full night by now and in the wide-eyed glare of the headlamps successive stands of unleaving fright-trees loomed up suddenly before us and were as suddenly gone, collapsing off into the darkness on either side as if felled by the pressure of our passing. Claire was leaning so far forward her nose was almost touching the windscreen. The light rising from the dashboard like green gas gave to her face a spectral hue. I said she should let me drive. She said I was too drunk to drive. I said I was not drunk. She said I had finished the hip-flask, she had seen me empty it. I said it was no business of hers to rebuke me in this fashion. She wept again, shouting through her tears. I said that even drunk I would have been less of a danger driving than she was in this state. So it went on, hammer and tongs, tooth and nail, what you will. I gave as good, or as bad, as I got, reminding her, merely as a corrective, that for the best part, I mean the worst part – how imprecise the language is, how inadequate to its occasions – of the year that it took her mother to die, she had been conveniently abroad, pursuing her studies, while I was left to cope as best I could.

This struck home. She gave a hoarse bellow between clenched teeth and thumped the heels of her hands on the wheel. Then she started to fling all sorts of accusations at me. She said I had *driven Jerome away*. I paused. Jerome? Jerome? She meant of course the chinless do-gooder – fat lot of good he did her – and sometime object of her affections. Jerome, yes, that was the scoundrel's unlikely name. How, pray, I asked, controlling myself, how had I *driven him away*? To that she replied only with a head-tossing snort. I pondered. It was true I had considered him an unsuitable suitor, and had told him so, pointedly, on more than one occasion, but she spoke as if I had brandished a horsewhip or let fly with a shotgun. Besides, if it was my opposition that had *driven him away*, what did that say for his character or his tenacity of purpose? No no, she was better off free of the likes of him, that was certain. But for now I said nothing more, kept my counsel, and after a mile or two the fire in her went out. That is something I have always found with women, wait long enough and one will have one's way.

When we got home I went straight into the house, leaving her to park the car, and got the number of the Cedars from the telephone book and telephoned Miss Vavasour and told her that I wished to rent one of her rooms. Then I went upstairs and crawled into bed in my drawers. I was suddenly very tired. A fight with one's daughter is never less than debilitating. I had moved by then from what had been Anna's and my bedroom into the spare room over the kitchen, which used to be the nursery and where the bed was low and narrow, hardly more than a cot. I could hear Claire below in the kitchen, banging the pots and pans. I had not told her yet that I had decided to sell the house. Miss V. on the telephone had enquired how long I planned to stay. I could hear from her tone that she was puzzled, even distrustful. I maintained a deliberate vagueness. Some weeks, I said, months, perhaps. She was silent for a lengthy moment, thinking. She mentioned the Colonel, he was a permanent, she said, and set in his ways. I volunteered no comment on that. What were colonels to me? She could entertain an entire officer corps on the premises for all I cared. She said I would have to send out my laundry. I asked her if she remembered me. 'Oh, yes,' she said without inflexion, 'yes, of course, I remember you.'

I heard Claire's step on the stairs. Her anger had drained all away by now and she walked at a dragging, disconsolate plod. I do not doubt she too finds arguments tiring. The bedroom door was ajar but she did not come in, only asked listlessly through the gap if I wanted something to eat. I had not switched on the lamps in the room and the long, tapering trapezoid of light spilling across the linoleum from the landing where she stood was a pathway leading straight to childhood, hers and my own. When she was little and slept in this room, in this bed, she liked to hear the sound of my typewriter from the study downstairs. It was a comforting sound, she said, like listening to me think, although I do not know how the sound of me thinking could comfort anyone; quite the opposite, I should have said. Ah, but how far off, now, those days, those nights. All the same, she should not have shouted at me like that in the car. I do not merit being shouted at like that. 'Daddy,' she said again, with a note of testiness now, 'do you want dinner or not?' I did not answer, and she went away. Live in the past, do I.

I turned towards the wall and away from the light. Even though my knees were bent my feet still stuck out at the end of the bed. As I was heaving myself over in a tangle of sheets – I have never been able to cope with bedclothes – I caught a whiff of my own warm cheesy smell. Before Anna's illness I had held my physical self in no more than fond disgust, as most people do – hold their selves, I mean, not mine – tolerant, necessarily, of the products of my sadly inescapable humanity, the various effluvia, the eructations fore and aft, the gleet, the scurf, the sweat and other common leakages, and even what the Bard of Hartford quaintly calls the particles of nether-do. However, when Anna's body betrayed her and she became afraid of it and its alien possibilities, I developed, by a mysterious process of transference, a crawling repugnance of my own flesh. I do not have this sense of self-disgust all the time, or at least I am not all the time aware of it, although probably it is there, waiting until I am alone, at night, or in the early morning especially, when it rises around me like a miasma of marsh gas. I have developed too a queasy fascination with the processes of my body, the gradual ones, the way for instance my hair and my fingernails insistently keep growing, no matter what state I am in, what anguish I may be undergoing. It seems so inconsiderate, so heedless of circumstance, this relentless generation of matter that is already dead, in the same way that animals will keep going about their animal business, unaware or uncaring that their master sprawled on his cold bed upstairs with mouth agape and eyes glazed over will not be coming down, ever again, to dish out the kibble or take the key to that last tin of sardines.

Speaking of typewriters – I did, I mentioned a typewriter a minute ago – last night in a dream, it has just come back to me, I was trying to write my will on a machine that was lacking the word *I*. The letter *I*, that is, small and large.

Down here, by the sea, there is a special quality to the silence at night. I do not know if this is my doing, I mean if this quality is something I bring to the silence of my room, and even of the whole house, or if it is a local effect, due to the salt in the air, perhaps, or the seaside climate in general. I do not recall noticing it when I was young and staying in the Field. It is dense and at the same time hollow. It took me a long while, nights and nights, to identify what it reminds me of. It is like the silence that I knew in the sickrooms of my childhood, when I would lie in a fever, cocooned under a hot, moist mound of blankets, with the emptiness squeezing in on my eardrums like the air in a bathysphere. Sickness in those days was a special place, a place apart, where no one else could enter, not the doctor with his shiver-inducing stethoscope or even my mother when she put her cool hand on my burning brow. It is a place like the place where I feel that I am now, miles from anywhere, and anyone. I think of the others in the house, Miss Vavasour, and the Colonel, asleep in their rooms, and then I think perhaps they are not asleep, but lying awake, like me, glooming gaunt-eyed into the lead-blue darkness. Perhaps the one is thinking of the other, for the Colonel has an idea of our chatelaine, I am convinced of it. She, however, laughs at him behind his back, not entirely without fondness, calling him Colonel Blunder, or Our Brave Soldier. Some mornings her eyes are red-rimmed as if she had been crying in the night. Does she blame herself for all that happened and grieve for it still? What a little vessel of sadness we are, sailing in this muffled silence through the autumn dark.

It was at night especially that I thought about the Graces, as I lay in my narrow metal bed in the chalet under the open window, hearing the monotonously repeated ragged collapse of waves down on the beach, the solitary cry of a sleepless seabird and, sometimes, the distant rattling of a corncrake, and the faint, jazzy moanings of the dance band in the Golf Hotel playing a last slow waltz, and my mother and father in the front room fighting, as they did when they thought I was asleep, going at each other in a grinding undertone, every night, every night, until at last one night my father left us, never to return. But that was in winter, and somewhere else, and years off still. To keep from trying to hear what they were saying I distracted myself by making up dramas in which I rescued Mrs Grace from some great and general catastrophe, a shipwreck or a devastating storm, and sequestered her for safety in a cave, conveniently dry and warm, where in moonlight – the liner had gone down by now, the storm had abated – I tenderly helped her out of her sopping swimsuit and wrapped a towel around her phosphorescent nudity, and we lay down and she leaned her head on my arm and touched my face in gratitude and sighed, and so we went to sleep together, she and I, lapped about by the vast soft summer night.

In those days I was greatly taken with the gods. I am not speaking of God, the capitalised one, but the gods in general. Or the idea of the gods, that is, the possibility of the gods. I was a keen reader and had a fair knowledge of the Greek myths, although the personages in them were hard to keep track of, so frequently did they transform themselves and so various were their adventures. Of them I had a necessarily stylised image – big, nearly naked plasticene figures all corded muscle and breasts like inverted tun-dishes – derived from the works of the great masters of the Italian Renaissance, Michelangelo especially, reproductions of whose paintings I must have seen in a book, or a magazine, I who was always on the look-out for instances of bare flesh. It was of course the erotic exploits of these celestial beings that most took my fancy. The thought of all that tensed and tensely quivering naked flesh, untrammelled save by the marmoreal folds of a robe or a wisp of gauze fortuitously placed – fortuitous, perhaps, but fully and frustratingly as protective of modesty as Rose's beach towel or, indeed, Connie Grace's swimsuit – glutted my inexperienced but already overheating imagination with reveries of love and love's transgressions, all in the unvarying form of pursuit and capture and violent overmastering. Of the details of these skirmishes in the golden dust of Greece I had scant grasp. I pictured the pump and shudder of tawny thighs from which pale loins shrink even as they surrender, and heard the moans of mingled ecstasy and sweet distress. The mechanics of the act, however, were beyond me. Once on my rambles along the thistled pathways of the Burrow, as that strip of scrubland between the seashore and the fields was called, I almost stumbled over a couple lying in a shallow sandy pit making love under a raincoat.

Their exertions had caused the coat to ride up, so that it covered their heads but not their tails – or perhaps they had arranged it that way, preferring to conceal their faces, so much more identifiable, after all, than behinds – and the sight of them there, the man's flanks rhythmically busy in the upright wishbone of the woman's lifted, wide-flung legs, made something swell and thicken in my throat, a blood-surge of alarm and thrilled revulsion. *So this*, I thought, or it was thought for me, *so this is what they do.*

Love among the big people. It was strange to picture them, to try to picture them, struggling together on their Olympian beds in the dark of night with only the stars to see them, grasping and clasping, panting endearments, crying out for pleasure as if in pain. How did they justify these dark deeds to their daytime selves? That was something that puzzled me greatly. Why were they not ashamed? On Sunday morning, say, they arrive at church still tingling from Saturday night's frolics. The priest greets them in the porch, they smile blamelessly, mumbling innocuous words. The woman dips her fingertips in the font, mingling traces of tenacious love-juice with the holy water. Under their Sunday best their thighs chafe in remembered delight. They kneel, not minding the mournfully reproachful gaze the statue of their Saviour fixes on them from the cross. After their midday Sunday dinner perhaps they will send the children out to play and retire to the sanctuary of their curtained bedroom and do it all over again, unaware of my mind's bloodshot eye fixed on them unblinkingly. Yes, I was that kind of boy. Or better say, there is part of me still that is the kind of boy that I was then. A little brute, in other words, with a filthy mind. As if there were any other sort. We never grow up. I never did, anyway.

By day I loitered about Station Road hoping for a glimpse of Mrs Grace. I would pass by the green metal gate, slowing to the pace of a somnambulist, and will her to walk out of the front door as her husband had walked out that day when I caught my first sight of him, but she kept stubbornly within. In desperation I would peer past the house to the clothesline in the garden, but all I saw was the children's laundry, their shorts and socks and one or two items of Chloe's uninterestingly skimpy under-things, and of course their father's flaccid, greyish drawers, and once, even, his sand-bucket hat, pegged at a rakish angle. The only thing of Mrs Grace's I ever saw there was her black swimsuit, hanging by its shoulder straps, limp and scandalously empty, dry now and less like a sealskin than the pelt of a panther. I looked in at the windows, too, especially the bedroom ones upstairs, and was rewarded one day – how my heart hammered! – by a glimpse behind a shadowed pane of what seemed a nude thigh that could only be hers. Then the adored flesh moved and turned into the hairy shoulder of her husband, at stool, for all I knew, and reaching for the lavatory roll.

There was a day when the door did open, but it was Rose who came out, and gave me a look that made me lower my eyes and hurry on. Yes, Rose had the measure of me from the start. Still has, no doubt.

I determined to get into the house, to walk where Mrs Grace walked, sit where she sat, touch the things that she touched. To this end I set about making the acquaintance of Chloe and her brother. It was easy, as these things were in childhood, even for a child as circumspect as I was. At that age we had no small-talk, no rituals of polite advance and encounter, but simply put ourselves into each other's vicinity and waited to see what would happen. I saw the two of them loitering on the gravel outside the Strand Café one day, spied them before they spied me, and crossed the road diagonally to where they were standing, and stopped. Myles was eating an ice cream with deep concentration, licking it evenly on all sides like a cat licking a kitten, while Chloe, I suppose having finished hers, waited on him in an attitude of torpid boredom, leaning in the doorway of the café with one sandalled foot pressed on the instep of the other and her face blankly lifted to the sunlight. I did not say anything, nor did they. The three of us just stood there in the morning sunshine amid smells of seawrack and vanilla and what passed in the Strand Café for coffee, and at last Chloe deigned to lower her head and directed her gaze towards my knees and asked my name. When I told her she repeated it, as if it were a suspect coin she was testing between her teeth.

'Morden?' she said. 'What sort of a name is that?'

We walked slowly up Station Road, Chloe and I in front and Myles behind us, gambolling, I nearly said, at our heels. They were from the city, Chloe said. That would not have been hard for me to guess. She asked where I was staying. I gestured vaguely.

'Down there,' I said. 'Along past the church.'

'In a house or a hotel?'

How quick she was. I considered lying – 'The Golf Hotel, actually' – but saw where a lie could lead me.

'A chalet,' I said, mumbling.

She nodded thoughtfully.

'I've always wanted to stay in a chalet,' she said.

This was no comfort to me. On the contrary, it caused me to have a momentary but starkly clear image of the crooked little wooden outhouse standing amid the lupins across from my bedroom window, and even seemed to catch a dry, woody whiff of the torn-up squares of newsprint impaled on their rusty nail just inside the door.

We came to the Cedars, stopped at the gate. The car was parked on the gravel. It had been out recently, the cooling engine was still clicking its tongue to itself in fussy complaint. I could hear faintly from inside the house the melting-toffee tones of a palm court orchestra playing on the wireless, and I pictured Mrs Grace and her husband dancing together in there, sweeping around the furniture, she with her head thrown back and her throat bared and he mincing on his satyr's furred hind legs and grinning up eagerly into her face – he was shorter than she by an inch or two – with all his sharp little teeth on show and his ice-blue eyes alight with mirthful lust. Chloe was tracing patterns in the gravel with the toe of her sandal. There were fine white hairs on her calves but her shins were smooth and shiny as stone. Suddenly Myles gave a little jump, or skip, as if for joy but too mechanical for that, like a clockwork figure coming abruptly to life, and clipped me playfully on the back of the head with his open palm and turned and with a gagging laugh scrambled agilely over the bars of the gate and dropped down to the gravel on the other side and spun about to face us and crouched with knees and elbows flexed, like an acrobat inviting his due of applause. Chloe made a face, pulling her mouth down at one side.

'Don't mind him,' she said in a tone of bored irritation. 'He can't talk.'

They were twins. I had never encountered twins before, in the flesh, and was fascinated and at the same time slightly repelled. There seemed to me something almost indecent in such a predicament. True, they were brother and sister and so could not be identical – the very thought of identical twins sent a shiver of secret and mysterious excitement along my spine – but still there must be between them an awful depth of intimacy. How would it be? Like having one mind and two bodies? If so it was almost disgusting to think of. Imagine somehow knowing intimately, from the inside, as it were, what another's body is like, its different parts, different smells, different urges. How, how would it be? I itched to know. In the makeshift picture-house one wet

Sunday afternoon – here I leap ahead – we were watching a film in which two convicts from a chain-gang made their escape still manacled together, and beside me Chloe stirred and made a muffled sound, a sort of laughing sigh. 'Look,' she whispered, 'it's me and Myles.' I was taken aback, and felt myself blush and was glad of the dark. She might have been admitting to something intimate and shameful. Yet it was the very notion of an impropriety in such close-ness that made me eager to know more, eager, and yet loath. Once – this is an even longer leap forward – when I got up the nerve to ask Chloe straight out to tell me, because I longed to know, what it felt like, this state of unavoidable intimacy with her brother – her other! – she thought for a moment and then held up her hands before her face, the palms pressed almost together but not quite touching. 'Like two magnets,' she said, 'but turned the wrong way, pulling and pushing.' After she had said it she fell darkly silent, as though this time it was she who thought she had let drop a shaming secret, and she turned away from me, and I felt for a moment something of the same panicky dizziness that I did when I held my breath for too long underwater. She was never less than alarming, was Chloe.

The link between them was palpable. I pictured

it as an invisibly fine thread of sticky shiny stuff, like spider's silk, or a glistening filament such as a snail might leave hanging as it crossed from one leaf to another, or steely and bright, it might be, and taut, like a harp-string, or a garotte. They were tied to each other, tied and bound. They felt things in common, pains, emotions, fears. They shared thoughts. They would wake in the night and lie listening to each other breathing, knowing they had been dreaming the same thing. They did not tell each other what was in the dream. There was no need. They knew.

Myles had been mute from birth. Or rather, simply, he had never spoken. The doctors could find no cause that would account for his stubborn silence, and professed themselves baffled, or sceptical, or both. At first it had been assumed he was a late starter and that in time he would begin to speak like everyone else, but the years went on and still he said not a word. Whether he had the ability to speak and chose not to, no one seemed to know. Was he mute or silent, silent or mute? Could he have a voice that he never used? Did he practise when there was no one to hear? I imagined him at night, in bed, under the covers, whispering to himself and smiling that avid, elfin smile of his. Or maybe he talked to Chloe. How they would have laughed, forehead to forehead and their arms thrown around each other's neck, sharing their secret.

'He'll talk when he has something to say,' his father would growl, with his accustomed menacing cheeriness.

It was plain that Mr Grace did not care for his son. He avoided him when he could, and was especially unwilling to be alone with him. This was no wonder, for being alone with Myles was like being in a room which someone had just violently left. His muteness was a pervasive and cloying emanation. He said nothing but was never silent. He was always fidgeting with things, snatching them up and immediately throwing them down again with a clatter. He made dry little clicking noises at the back of his throat. One heard him breathe.

His mother treated him with a sort of trailing vagueness. At moments as she weaved abstractedly through her day – although she was not a serious drinker she always looked to be mellowly a little drunk – she would stop and seem to notice him with not quite recognition, and would frown and smile at the same time, in a rueful, helpless fashion.

Neither parent could do proper sign language, and spoke to Myles by way of an improvised, brusque dumb-show that seemed less an attempt at communication than an impatient waving of him out of their sight. Yet he understood well enough what it was they were trying to say, and often before they were halfway through trying to say it, which only made them more impatient and irritated with him. Deep down they were both, I am sure, a little afraid of him. That is no wonder either. It must have been like living with an all too visible, all too tangible poltergeist.

For my part, although I am ashamed to say it, or at least I should be ashamed, what Myles put me most in mind of was a dog I once had, an irrepressibly enthusiastic terrier of which I was greatly fond but which on occasion, when there was no one about, I would cruelly beat, poor Pongo, for the hot, tumid pleasure I derived from its yelps of pain and its supplicatory squirmings. What twig-like fingers Myles had, what brittle, girlish wrists! He would goad me, plucking at my sleeve, or walking on my heels and popping his grinning head repeatedly up from under my arm, until at last I would turn on him and knock him down, which was easy to do, for I was big and strong even then, and taller than he was by a head. When he was down, however, there was the question of what to do with him, since unless prevented he would be up again at once, rolling over himself like one of those self-righting toy figures and springing effortlessly back on to his toes. When I sat on his chest I could feel the wobble of his heart against my groin, his ribcage straining and the fluttering of the taut, concave integument below his breast-bone, and he would laugh up at me, panting, and showing his moist, useless tongue. But was not I too a little afraid of him, in my heart, or wherever it is that fear resides?

In accordance with the mysterious protocols of childhood – were we children? I think there should be another word for what we were – they did not invite me into the house that first time, after I had accosted them outside the Strand Café. In fact, I do not recall under what circumstances exactly I managed eventually to get inside the Cedars. I see myself after that initial encounter turning away frustratedly from the green gate with the twins watching me go, and then I see myself another day within the very sanctum itself, as if, by a truly magical version of Myles's leap over the top bar of the gate, I had vaulted all obstacles to land up in the living room next to an angled, solid-seeming beam of brassy sunlight, with Mrs Grace in a loose-fitting, flowered dress, light-blue with a darker pattern of blue blossoms, turning from a table and smiling at me, deliberately vague, evidently not knowing who I was but knowing nevertheless that she should, which shows that this cannot have been the first time we had encountered each other face to face. Where was Chloe? Where was Myles? Why was I left alone with their mother? She asked if I would like something, a glass of lemonade, perhaps. 'Or,' she said in a tone of faint desperation, 'an apple . . . ?' I shook my head. Her proximity, the mere fact of her thereness, filled me with excitement and a mysterious sort of sorrow. Who knows the pangs that pierce a small boy's heart? She put her head on one side, puzzled, and amused, too, I could see, by the tongue-tied intensity of my presence before her. I must have seemed like a moth throbbing before a candle-flame, or like the flame itself, shivering in its own consuming heat.

What was it she had been doing at the table? Arranging flowers in a vase – or is that too fanciful? There is a multi-coloured patch in my memory of the moment, a shimmer of variegated brightness where her hands hover. Let me linger here with her a little while, before Rose appears, and Myles and Chloe return from wherever they are, and her goatish husband comes clattering on to the scene; she will be displaced soon enough from the throbbing centre of my attentions. How intensely that sunbeam glows.

Where is it coming from? It has an almost churchly cast, as if, impossibly, it were slanting down from a rose window high above us. Beyond the smouldering sunlight there is the placid gloom of indoors on a summer afternoon, where my memory gropes in search of details, solid objects, the components of the past. Mrs Grace, Constance, Connie, is still smiling at me in that unfocused way, which, now that I consider it, is how she looked at everything, as if she were not absolutely persuaded of the world's solidity and half expected it all at any moment to turn, in some outlandish and hilarious way, into something entirely different.

I would have said then that she was beautiful, had there been anyone to whom I would have thought of saying such a thing, but I suppose she was not, really. She was rather stocky, and her hands were fat and reddish, there was a bump at the tip of her nose, and the two lank strands of blonde hair that her fingers kept pushing back behind her ears and that kept falling forward again were darker than the rest of her hair and had the slightly greasy hue of oiled oak. She walked at a languorous slouch, the muscles in her haunches quivering under the light stuff of her summer dresses. She smelled of sweat and cold cream and, faintly, of cooking fat. Just another woman, in other words, and another mother, at that. Yet to me she was in all her ordinariness as remote and remotely desirable as any a painted pale lady with unicorn and book. But no, I should be fair to myself, child though I was, nascent romantic though I may have been. She was, even for me, not pale, she was not made of paint. She was wholly real, thick-meated, edible, almost. This was the most remarkable thing of all, that she was at once a wraith of my imagination and a woman of unavoidable flesh and blood, of fibre and musk and milk. My hitherto hardly less than seemly dreams of rescue and amorous dalliance had by now become riotous fantasies, vivid and at the same time hopelessly lacking in essential detail, of being voluptuously overborne by her, of sinking to the ground under all her warm weight, of being rolled, of being ridden, between her thighs, my arms pinned against my breast and my face on fire, at once her demon lover and her child.

At times the image of her would spring up in me unbidden, an interior succubus, and a surge of yearning would engorge the very root of my being. One greenish twilight after rain, with a wedge of wet sunlight in the window and an impossibly unseasonal thrush piping outside in the dripping lupins, I lay face down on my bed in such an intense suffusion of unassuageable desire – it hovered, this desire, like a nimbus about the image of my beloved, enfolding her everywhere and nowhere focused – that I broke into sobs, lavish, loud and thrillingly beyond all control. My mother heard me and came into the room, but said nothing, uncharacteristically – I might have expected a brusque interrogation, followed by a smack – only picked up a pillow that the thrashings of my grief had pushed off the bed and, after the briefest of hesitations, went out again, shutting the door soundlessly behind her. What did she imagine I was weeping for, I wondered, and wonder again now. Had she somehow recognised my rapturously lovesick grief for what it was? I could not believe it. How would she, who was merely my mother, know anything of this storm of passion in which I was helplessly suspended, the frail wings of my emotions burned and blasted by love's relentless flame? Oh, Ma, how little I understood you, thinking how little you understood.

So there I am, in that Edenic moment at what was suddenly the centre of the world, with that shaft of sunlight and those vestigial flowers – sweet pea? all at once I seem to see sweet pea – and blonde Mrs Grace offering me an apple that was however nowhere in evidence, and everything about to be interrupted with a grinding of cogwheels and a horrible, stomach-turning lurch. All sorts of things began to happen at once. Through an open doorway a small black woolly dog came skittering in from outside – somehow now the action has shifted from the living room to the kitchen – its nails making frantic skittling noises on the pitchpine floor. It had a tennis ball in its mouth. Immediately Myles appeared in pursuit, with Rose in turn pursuing him. He tripped or pretended to trip over a rucked rug and pitched forward only to tumble nimbly head over heel and leap to his feet again, almost knocking into his mother, who gave a cry in which were mingled startlement and weary annoyance – 'For heaven's sake, Myles!' – while the dog, its pendent ears flapping, changed tack and shot underneath the table, still grinningly gripping the ball. Rose made a feint at the animal but it dodged aside. Now through another doorway, like Old Father Time himself, came Carlo Grace, wearing shorts and sandals and with a big beach towel draped over his shoulders, his hairy paunch on show. At sight of Myles and the dog he gave a roar of sham rage and stamped his foot threateningly, and the dog let go of the ball, and dog and boy disappeared through the door as precipitately as they had entered. Rose laughed, a high whinny, and looked quickly at Mrs Grace and bit her lip. The door banged and in rapid echo another door banged upstairs, where a lavatory, flushed a moment previously, had set up its after-gulps and gurglings. The ball that the dog had dropped rolled slowly, shiny with spit, into the middle of the floor. Mr Grace, seeing me, a stranger – he must have forgotten that day of the wink – mugged a double-take, throwing back his head and screwing up his face at one side and sighting quizzically at me along the side of his nose. I heard Chloe coming downstairs, her sandals slapping on the steps. By the time she entered the room Mrs Grace had introduced me to her husband – I think it was the first time in my life I had been formally introduced to anyone, although I had to say my name since Mrs Grace had still not remembered it – and he was shaking my hand with a show of mock solemnity, addressing me as *My dear sir!* and putting on a cockney accent and declaring that any friend of his children's would always be welcome in *our 'umble 'ome*. Chloe rolled her eyes and gave a shuddering gasp of disgust. 'Shut *up*, Daddy,' she said through clenched teeth, and he, feigning terror of her, let go my hand and drew the towel shawl-like over his head and hurried at a crouch on tiptoe out of the room, making little bat-squeaks of pretend

91

fright and dismay. Mrs Grace was lighting a cigarette. Chloe without even a glance in my direction crossed the room to the door where her father had gone out. 'I need a lift!' she shouted after him. 'I need—' The car door slammed, the engine started, the big tyres mashed the gravel. 'Damn,' Chloe said.

Mrs Grace was leaning against the table – the one with the sweet pea on it, for magically we are back in the living room again – smoking her cigarette in the way that women did in those days, one arm folded across her midriff and the elbow of the other cupped in a palm. She lifted an eyebrow at me and smiled wryly and shrugged, picking a fleck of tobacco from her lower lip. Rose stooped and wrinkling her nose picked up reluctantly the spit-smeared ball between a finger and thumb. Outside the gate the car horn tooted merrily twice and we heard the car drive away. The dog was barking wildly, wanting to be let in again to retrieve the ball.

By the way, that dog. I never saw it again. Whose can it have been?

Odd sense of lightness today, of, what shall I call it, of volatility. The wind is up again, it is fairly blowing a tempest out there, which must be the cause of this giddiness I am feeling. For I have always been strongly susceptible to the weather and its effects. As a child I loved to curl up by the wireless set of a winter eve and listen to the shipping forecast, picturing all those doughty sea-dogs in their sou'westers battling through house-high waves in Fogger and Disher and Jodrell Bank, or whatever those far-flung sea areas are called. Often as an adult, too, I would have that same feeling, there with Anna in our fine old house between the mountains and the sea, when the autumn gales groaned in the chimneys and the waves were coming over the sea wall in washes of boiling white spume. Before the pit opened under our feet that day in Mr Todd's rooms – which, come to think of it, did have about them something of the air of a sinisterly superior barber's shop – I was often surprised to ponder how many of life's good things had been granted me. If that child dreaming by the wireless had been asked what he wanted to be when he grew up, what I had become was more or less what he would have described, in however halting a fashion, I am sure of it. This is remarkable, I think, even allowing for my present sorrows. Are not the majority of men disappointed with their lot, languishing in quiet desperation in their chains?

I wonder if other people when they were children

had this kind of image, at once vague and particular, of what they would be like when they grew up. I am not speaking of hopes and aspirations, vague ambitions, that kind of thing. From the outset I was very precise and definite in my expectations. I did not want to be an engine driver or a famous explorer. When I peered wishfully through the mists from the all too real then to the blissfully imagined now, this is, as I have said, exactly how I would have foreseen my future self, a man of leisurely interests and scant ambition sitting in a room just like this one, in my sea-captain's chair, leaning at my little table, in just this season, the year declining towards its end in clement weather, the leaves scampering, the brightness imperceptibly fading from the days and the street lamps coming on only a fraction earlier each evening. Yes, this is what I thought adulthood would be, a kind of long indian summer, a state of tranquillity, of calm incuriousness, with nothing left of the barely bearable raw immediacy of childhood, all the things solved that had puzzled me when I was small, all mysteries settled, all questions answered, and the moments dripping away, unnoticed almost, drip by golden drip, towards the final, almost unnoticed, quietus.

There were things of course the boy that I was

then would not have allowed himself to foresee, in his eager anticipations, even if he had been able. Loss, grief, the sombre days and the sleepless nights, such surprises tend not to register on the prophetic imagination's photographic plate.

And then, too, when I consider the matter closely, I see that the version of the future that I pictured as a boy had an oddly antique cast to it. The world in which I live now would have been, in my imagining of it then, for all my perspicacity, different from what it is in fact, but subtly different; would have been, I see, all slouched hats and crombie overcoats and big square motor cars with winged manikins bounding from the bonnets. When had I known such things, that I could figure them so distinctly? I think it is that, being unable to conceive exactly what the future would look like but certain that I would be a person of some eminence in it, I must have furnished it with the trappings of success as I saw it among the great folk of our town, the doctors and solicitors, the provincial industrialists for whom my father humbly worked, the few remnants of Protestant gentry still clinging on in their Big Houses down the bosky side roads of the town's hinterland.

But no, that is not it either. It does not adequately account for the genteelly outmoded atmosphere that pervaded my dream of what was to come. The precise images I entertained of myself as a grown-up – seated, say, in three-piece pinstriped suit and raked fedora in the back seat of my chauffered Humber Hawk with a blanket over my knees – were imbued, I realise, with that etiolated, world-weary elegance, that infirm poise, which I associated, or which at least I associate now, with a time before the time of my childhood, that recent antiquity which was, of course, yes, the world between the wars. So what I foresaw for the future was in fact, if fact comes into it, a picture of what could only be an imagined past. I was, one might say, not so much anticipating the future as nostalgic for it, since what in my imaginings was to come was in reality already gone. And suddenly now this strikes me as in some way significant. Was it actually the future I was looking forward to, or something beyond the future?

The truth is, it has all begun to run together, past and possible future and impossible present. In the ashen weeks of daytime dread and nightly terror before Anna was forced at last to acknowledge the inevitability of Mr Todd and his prods and potions, I seemed to inhabit a twilit netherworld in which it was scarcely possible to distinguish dream from waking, since both waking and dreaming had the same penetrable, darkly velutinous texture, and in which I was wafted this way and that in a state of feverish lethargy, as if it were I and not Anna who was destined soon to be another one among the already so numerous shades. It was a gruesome version of that phantom pregnancy I experienced when Anna first knew she was expecting Claire; now it seemed I was suffering a phantom illness along with her. On all sides there were portents of mortality. I was plagued by coincidences; long-forgotten things were suddenly remembered; objects turned up that for years had been lost. My life seemed to be passing before me, not in a flash as it is said to do for those about to drown, but in a sort of leisurely convulsion, emptying itself of its secrets and its quotidian mysteries in preparation for the moment when I must step into the black boat on the shadowed river with the coin of passage cold in my already coldening hand. Strange as it was, however, this imagined place of pre-departure was not entirely unfamiliar to me. On occasion in the past, in moments of inexplicable transport, in my study, perhaps, at my desk, immersed in words, paltry as they may be, for even the second-rater is sometimes inspired, I had felt myself break through the membrane of mere consciousness into another state, one which had no name, where ordinary laws did not operate, where time moved differently if it moved at all, where I was neither alive nor the other thing and yet more vividly present than ever I could be in what we call, because we must, the real world. And even years before that again, standing for instance with Mrs Grace in that sunlit living room, or sitting with Chloe in the dark of the picture-house, I was there and not there, myself and revenant, immured in the moment and yet hovering somehow on the point of departure. Perhaps all of life is no more than a long preparation for the leaving of it.

For Anna in her illness the nights were worst. That was only to be expected. So many things were only to be expected, now that the ultimate unexpected had arrived. In the dark all the breathless incredulity of daytime – *this cannot be happening to me!* – gave way in her to a dull, unmoving amazement. As she lay sleepless beside me I could almost feel her fear, spinning steadily inside her, like a dynamo. At moments in the dark she would laugh out loud, it was a sort of laugh, in renewed sheer surprise at the fact of this plight into which she had been so pitilessly, so ignominiously, delivered. Mostly, however, she kept herself quiet, lying on her side curled up like a lost explorer in his tent, half in a doze, half in a daze, indifferent equally, it seemed, to the prospect of survival or extinction. Up to now all her experiences had been temporary. Griefs had been assuaged, if only by time, joys had hardened into habit, her body had cured its own minor maladies. This, however, this was an absolute, a singularity, an end in itself, and yet she could not grasp it, could not absorb it. If there were pain, she said, it would at least be an authenticator, the thing to tell her that what had happened to her was realler than any reality she had known before now. But she was not in pain, not yet; there was only what she described as a general sense of agitation, a sort of interior fizzing, as if her poor, baffled body were scrabbling about inside itself, desperately throwing up defences against an invader that had already scuttled in by a secret way, its shiny black pincers snapping.

In those endless October nights, lying side by side in the darkness, toppled statues of ourselves, we sought escape from an intolerable present in the only tense possible, the past, that is, the faraway past. We went back over our earliest days together, reminding, correcting, helping each other, like two ancients tottering arm-in-arm along the ramparts of a town where they had once lived, long ago.

We recalled especially the smoky London summer

in which we met and married. I spotted Anna first at a party in someone's flat one chokingly hot afternoon, all the windows wide open and the air blue with exhaust fumes from the street outside and the honking of passing buses sounding incongruously like fog horns through the clamour and murk in the crowded rooms. It was the size of her that first caught my attention. Not that she was so very large, but she was made on a scale different from that of any woman I had known before her. Big shoulders, big arms, big feet, that great head with its sweep of thick dark hair. She was standing between me and the window, in cheesecloth and sandals, talking to another woman, in that way that she had, at once intent and remote, dreamily twisting a lock of hair around a finger, and for a moment my eye had difficulty fixing a depth of focus, since it seemed that, of the two of them, Anna, being so much the bigger, must be much nearer to me than the one to whom she was speaking.

Ah, those parties, so many of them in those days. When I think back I always see us arriving, pausing together on the threshold for a moment, my hand on the small of her back, touching through brittle silk the cool deep crevice there, her wild smell in my nostrils and the heat of her hair against my cheek.

How grand we must have looked, the two of us, making our entrance, taller than everyone else, our gaze directed over their heads as if fixed on some far fine vista that only we were privileged enough to see.

At the time she was trying to become a photographer, taking moody early-morning studies, all soot and raw silver, of some of the bleaker corners of the city. She wanted to work, to do something, to be someone. The East End called to her, Brick Lane, Spitalfields, such places. I never took any of this seriously. Perhaps I should have. She lived with her father in a rented apartment in a liver-coloured mansion on one of those gloomy backwaters off Sloane Square. It was an enormous place, with a succession of vast, high-ceilinged rooms and tall sash-windows that seemed to avert their glazed gaze from the mere human spectacle passing back and forth between them. Her Daddy, old Charlie Weiss – 'Don't worry, it's not a Jew name' – took to me at once. I was big and young and gauche, and my presence in those gilded rooms amused him. He was a merry little man with tiny delicate hands and tiny feet. His wardrobe was an amazement to me, innumerable Savile Row suits, shirts from Charvet in cream and bottle-green and aquamarine silk, dozens of pairs of handmade miniature shoes. His head, which he took to Trumper's to be shaved every other day – hair, he said, is fur, no human being should tolerate it – was a perfect polished egg, and he wore those big heavy spectacles favoured by tycoons of the time, with flanged ear-pieces and lenses the size of saucers in which his sharp little eyes darted like inquisitive, exotic fish. He could not be still, jumping up and sitting down and then jumping up again, seeming, under those lofty ceilings, a tiny burnished nut rattling around inside an outsized shell. On my first visit he showed me proudly around the flat, pointing out the pictures, old masters every one, so he imagined, the giant television set housed in a walnut cabinet, the bottle of Dom Perignon and basket of flawless inedible fruit that had been sent him that day by a business associate – Charlie did not have friends, partners, clients, but only associates. Light of summer thick as honey fell from the tall windows and glowed on the figured carpets. Anna sat on a sofa with her chin on her hand and one leg folded under her and watched dispassionately as I negotiated my way around her preposterous little father. Unlike most small people he was not at all intimidated by us big ones, and seemed indeed to find my bulk reassuring, and kept pressing close up to me, almost amorously; there were moments, while he was displaying the gleaming fruits of his success, when it seemed that he might of a sudden hop up and settle himself all comfy in the cradle of my arms. When he had mentioned his business interests for the third time I asked what business it was that he was in and he turned on me a gaze of flawless candour, those twin fish-bowls flashing.

'Heavy machinery,' he said, managing not to laugh.

Charlie regarded the spectacle of his life with delight and a certain wonder at the fact of having got away so easily with so much. He was a crook, probably dangerous, and wholly, cheerfully immoral. Anna held him in fond and rueful regard. How such a diminutive man had got so mighty a daughter was a mystery. Young as she was she seemed the tolerant mother and he the waywardly winning manchild. Her own mother had died when Anna was twelve and since then father and daughter had faced the world like a pair of nineteenth-century adventurers, a riverboat gambler, say, and his alibi girl. There were parties at the flat two or three times a week, raucous occasions through which champagne flowed like a bubbling and slightly rancid river. One night towards the end of that summer we came back from the park – I liked to walk with her at dusk through the dusty shadows under the trees that were already beginning to make that fretful, dry, papery rustle that harbinges autumn – and before we had even turned into the street we heard the sounds of tipsy revelry from the flat. Anna put a hand on my arm and we stopped. Something in the air of evening bespoke a sombre promise. She turned to me and took one of the buttons of my jacket between a finger and thumb and twisted it forward and back like the dial of a safe, and in her usual mild and mildly preoccupied fashion invited me to marry her.

Throughout that expectant, heat-hazed summer I seemed to have been breathing off the shallowest top of my lungs, like a diver poised on the highest board above that tiny square of blue so impossibly far below. Now Anna had called up to me ringingly to *jump, jump!* Today, when only the lower orders and what remains of the gentry bother to marry, and everyone else takes a partner, as if life were a dance, or a business venture, it is perhaps hard to appreciate how vertiginous a leap it was back then to plight one's troth. I had plunged into the louche world of Anna and her father as if into another medium, a fantastical one wherein the rules as I had known them up to then did not apply, where everything shimmered and nothing was real, or was real but looked fake, like that platter of perfect fruit in Charlie's flat. Now I was being invited to become a denizen of these excitingly alien deeps. What Anna proposed to me, there in the dusty summer dusk on the corner of Sloane Street, was not so much marriage as the chance to fulfil the fantasy of myself.

The wedding party was held under a striped marquee in the mansion's unexpectedly spacious back garden. It was one of the last days of that summer's heat-wave, the air, like scratched glass, crazed by glinting sunlight. Throughout the afternoon long gleaming motor cars kept pulling up outside and depositing yet more guests, heron-like ladies in big hats and girls in white lipstick and white leather knee-high boots, raffish pinstriped gents, delicate young men who pouted and smoked pot, and lesser, indeterminate types, Charlie's business associates, sleek, watchful and unsmiling, in shiny suits and shirts with different-coloured collars and sharp-toed ankle-boots with elasticated sides. Charlie bounced about amongst them all, his blued pate agleam, pride pouring off him like sweat. Late in the day a huddle of warm-eyed, slow-moving, shy plump men in headdresses and spotless white djellabas arrived in our midst like a flock of doves. Later still a dumpy dowager in a hat got stridently drunk and fell down and had to be carried away in the arms of her stone-jawed chauffeur. As the light thickened in the trees and the shadow of the next-door house began to close over the garden like a trapdoor, and the last drunken couples in their clown-bright clothes were shuffling around the makeshift wooden dance floor one last time with their heads fallen on each other's shoulders and their eyes shut and eyelids fluttering, Anna and I stood on the tattered edges of it all, and a dark burst of starlings out of nowhere flew low over the marquee, their wings making a clatter that was like a sudden round of applause, exuberant and sarcastic.

Her hair. Suddenly I am thinking of her hair, the long dark lustrous coil of it falling away from her forehead in a sideways sweep. Even in her middle age there was hardly a strand of grey in it. We were driving home from the hospital one day when she lifted a length of it from her shoulder and held it close to her eyes and examined it strand by strand, frowning.

'Is there a bird called a baldicoot?' she asked.

'There is a bandicoot,' I said cautiously, 'but I don't think it's a bird. Why?'

'Apparently I shall be as bald as a coot in a month or two.'

'Who told you that?'

'A woman in the hospital who was having treatment, the kind I am to have. She was quite bald, so I suppose she would know.' For a while she watched the houses and the shops progressing past the car window in that stealthily indifferent way that they do, and then turned to me again. 'But what is a coot?'

'That's a bird.'

'Ah.' She chuckled. 'I'll be the spitting image of Charlie when it has all fallen out.'

She was.

He died, old Charlie, of a blood clot in the brain, a few months after we were married. Anna got all his money. There was not as much of it as I would have expected, but still, there was a lot.

The odd thing, one of the odd things, about my passion for Mrs Grace is that it fizzled out almost in the same moment that it achieved what might be considered its apotheosis. It all happened on the afternoon of the picnic. By then we were going about everywhere together, Chloe and Myles and I. How proud I was to be seen with them, these divinities, for I thought of course that they were the gods, so different were they from anyone I had hitherto known. My former friends in the Field, where I no longer played, were resentful of my desertion. 'He spends all his time now with his grand new friends,' I heard my mother one day telling one of their mothers. 'The boy, you know,' she added in an undertone, 'is a dummy.' To me she wondered why I did not petition the Graces to adopt me. 'I won't mind,' she said. 'Get you out from under my feet.' And she gave me a level look, harsh and unblinking, the same look she would often turn on me after my father had gone, as if to say, *I suppose you will be the next to betray me*. As I suppose I was.

My parents had not met Mr and Mrs Grace, nor would they. People in a proper house did not mix with people from the chalets, and we would not expect to mix with them. We did not drink gin, or have people down for the weekend, or leave touring maps of France insouciantly on show in the back windows of our motor cars – few in the Field even had a motor car. The social structure of our summer world was as fixed and hard of climbing as a ziggurat. The few families who owned holiday homes were at the top, then came those who could afford to put up at hotels – the Beach was more desirable than the Golf – then there were the house renters, and then us. All-the-year-rounders did not figure in this hierarchy; villagers in general, such as Duignan the dairyman or deaf Colfer the golf-ball collector, or the two Protestant spinsters at the Ivy Lodge, or the French woman who ran the tennis courts and was said to copulate regularly with her alsatian dog, all these were a class apart, their presence no more than the blurred background to our intenser, sun-shone-upon doings. That I had managed to scramble from the base of those steep social steps all the way up to the level of the Graces seemed, like my secret passion for Connie Grace, a token of specialness, of being the one chosen among so many of the unelect. The gods had singled me out for their favour.

The picnic. We went that afternoon in Mr Grace's racy motor car far down the Burrow, all the way to where the paved road ended. A note of the voluptuous had been struck immediately by the feel of the stippled leather of the seat cover sticking to the backs of my thighs below my shorts. Mrs Grace sat beside her husband in front, half turned towards him, an elbow resting on the back of her seat so that I had a view of her armpit, excitingly stubbled, and even caught now and then, when the breeze from the open window veered my way, a whiff of her sweat-dampened flesh's civet scent. She was wearing a garment which I believe even in those demurer days was called, with graphic frankness, a halter top, no more than a strapless white woollen tube, very tight, and very revealing of the curves of her bosom's heavy undersides. She had on her film star's sunglasses with the white frames and was smoking a fat cigarette. It excited me to watch as she took a deep drag and let her mouth hang open crookedly for a moment, a rich curl of smoke suspended motionless between those waxily glistening scarlet lips. Her fingernails too were painted a bright sanguineous red. I was seated directly behind her in the back seat, with Chloe in the middle between Myles and me. Chloe's hot, bony thigh was pressed negligently against my leg. Brother and sister were engaged in one of their private wordless contests, tussling and squirming, plucking at each other with pincer fingers and trying to kick each other's shins in the cramped space between the seats. I never could make out the rules of these games, if rules there were, although a winner always emerged in the end, Chloe, most often. I recall, with even now a faint stirring of pity for poor Myles, the first time I witnessed them playing in this way, or fighting, more like. It was a wet afternoon and we were trapped indoors at the Cedars. What savagery a rainy day could bring out in us children! The twins were sitting on the living-room floor, on their heels, facing each other, knee to knee, glaring into each other's eyes, their fingers interlocked, swaying and straining, intent as a pair of battling samurai, until at last something happened, I did not see what it was, although it was decisive, and Myles all at once was forced to surrender. Snatching his fingers from her steely claws he threw his arms around himself – he was a great clutcher of the injured or insulted self – and began to cry, in frustration and rage, emitting a high, strangled whine, his lower lip clamped over the upper and his eyes squeezed shut and spurting big, shapeless tears, the whole effect too dramatic to be entirely convincing. And what a gloatingly feline look victorious Chloe gave me over her shoulder, her face unpleasantly pinched and an eye-tooth glinting. Now, in the car, she won again, doing something to Myles's wrist that made him squeal. 'Oh, do stop, you two,' their mother said wearily, barely giving them a glance. Chloe, still grinning thinly in triumph, pressed her hip harder against my leg, while Myles grimaced, making a pursed O of his lips, this time holding back his tears, but barely, and chafing his reddened wrist.

At the end of the road Mr Grace stopped the car, and the hamper with its sandwiches and tea cups and bottles of wine was lifted from the boot and we set off to walk along a broad track of hard sand marked by an immemorial half-submerged rusted barbed-wire fence. I had never liked, even feared a little, this wild reach of marsh and mud flats where everything seemed turned away from the land, looking off desperately towards the horizon as if in mute search for a sign of rescue. The mud shone blue as a new bruise, and there were stands of bulrushes, and forgotten marker buoys tethered to slimed-over rotting wooden posts. High tide here was never more than inches deep, the water racing in over the flats swift and shiny as mercury, stopping at nothing. Mr Grace scampered ahead bandily, a folding chair clutched under each arm and that comical bucket hat tilted over his ear. We rounded the point and saw across the strait the town humped on its hill, a toy-like lavender jumble of planes and angles surmounted by a spire. Seeming to know where he was going Mr Grace struck off from the track into a meadow thronged with great tall ferns. We followed, Mrs Grace, Chloe, Myles, me. The ferns were as high as my head. Mr Grace was waiting for us on a grassy bank at the edge of the meadow, under an umbrella pine. Unnoticed, a shattered fern stalk had gouged a furrow in my bare ankle above the side of my sandal.

On a patch of grass between the low grassy bank and the wall of ferns a white cloth was spread. Mrs Grace, kneeling, a cigarette clamped in a corner of her mouth and one eye shut against the smoke, laid out the picnic things, while her husband, his hat falling further askew, struggled to draw a resistant wine cork. Myles was already off among the ferns. Chloe sat froglike on her haunches, eating an egg sandwich. Rose – where is Rose? She is there, in her scarlet shirt and dancing pumps and dancer's tight black pants with the straps that go under the soles of her feet, and her hair black as a crow's wing tied in a plume behind her fine-boned head. But how did she get here? She had not been in the car with us. A bicycle, yes, I see a bicycle asprawl in abandon among the ferns, handlebars turned sideways and its front wheel jutting up at a somehow unseemly angle, a sly prefiguring, as it seems now, of what was to come. Mr Grace clamped the wine bottle between his knees and strained and strained, his earlobes turning red. Behind me Rose sat down at one corner of the tablecloth, leaning on a braced arm, her cheek almost resting on her shoulder, her legs folded off to the side, in a pose that should have been awkward but was not. I could hear Myles running in the ferns. Suddenly the cork came out of

113

the wine bottle with a comical pop that startled us all.

We ate our picnic. Myles was pretending to be a wild beast and kept running in from the ferns and snatching handfuls of food and loping off again, hooting and whinnying. Mr and Mrs Grace drank their wine and presently Mr Grace was opening another bottle, this time with less difficulty. Rose said she was not hungry but Mrs Grace said that was nonsense and commanded her to eat and Mr Grace, grinning, offered her a banana. The afternoon was breezy under an as yet unclouded sky. The crooked pine soughed above us, and there was a smell of pine needles, and of grass and crushed ferns, and the salt tang of the sea. Rose sulked, I supposed because of Mrs Grace's rebuke and Mr Grace's offer of that lewd banana. Chloe was engrossed in picking at the stipples of a ruby cicatrice just below her elbow where the previous day a thorn had scratched her. I examined the fern-wound on my ankle, an angry pink groove between translucent deckle edges of whitish skin; it had not bled but in the deeps of the groove a clear ichor glinted. Mr Grace sat slumped into himself in a folding chair with one leg crossed on the other, smoking a cigarette, his hat pulled low on his forehead, shadowing his eyes.

I felt a soft small thing strike me on the cheek. Chloe had left off picking at her scabs and had thrown a breadcrumb at me. I looked at her and she looked back without expression and threw another crumb. This time she missed. I picked up the crumb from the grass and threw it back, but I missed, too. Mrs Grace was idly watching us, reclining on her side directly in front of me on the shallow incline of the verdant bank, her head supported on a hand. She had set the stem of her wine glass in the grass with the bowl wedged at an angle against a sideways lolling breast – I wondered, as so often, if they were not sore to carry, those big twin bulbs of milky flesh – and now she licked a fingertip and ran it around the rim of the glass, trying to make it sing, but no sound came. Chloe put a pellet of bread into her mouth and wetted it with spit and took it out again and kneaded it in her fingers with slow deliberation and took leisurely aim and threw it at me, but the wad fell short. 'Chloe!' her mother said, a wan reproach, and Chloe ignored her and smiled at me her cat's thin, gloating smile. She was a cruel-hearted girl, my Chloe. For her amusement of a day I would catch a handful of grasshoppers and tear off one of their back legs to prevent them escaping and put the twitching torsos in the lid of a polish tin and douse them in paraffin and set them alight. How intently, squatting with hands pressed on her knees, she would watch the unfortunate creatures as they seethed, boiling in their own fat.

She was making another spit-ball. 'Chloe, you are disgusting,' Mrs Grace said with a sigh, and Chloe, all at once bored, spat out the bread and brushed the crumbs from her lap and rose and walked off sulkily into the shadow of the pine tree.

Did Connie Grace catch my eye? Was that a complicit smile? With a heaving sigh she turned and lay down supine on the bank with her head leaning back on the grass and flexed one leg, so that suddenly I was allowed to see under her skirt along the inner side of her thigh all the way up to the hollow of her lap and the plump mound there sheathed in tensed white cotton. At once everything began to slow. Her emptied glass fell over in a swoon and a last drop of wine ran to the rim and hung an instant glittering and then fell. I stared and stared, my brow growing hot and my palms wet. Mr Grace under his hat seemed to be smirking at me but I did not care, he could smirk all he liked. His big wife, growing bigger by the moment, a foreshortened, headless giantess at whose huge feet I crouched in what felt almost like fear, gave a sort of wriggle and raised her knee higher still, revealing the crescent-shaped crease at the full-fleshed back of her leg where her rump began. A drumbeat in my temples was making the daylight dim. I was aware of the throbbing sting in my gouged ankle. And now from far off in the ferns there came a thin, shrill sound, an archaic pipe-note piercing through the lacquered air, and Chloe, up at the tree, scowled as if called to duty and bent and plucked a blade of grass and pressing it between her thumbs blew an answering note out of the conch-shell of her cupped hands.

After a timeless minute or two my sprawling maja drew in her leg and turned on her side again and fell asleep with shocking suddenness – her gentle snores were the sound of a small, soft engine trying and failing repeatedly to start – and I sat up, carefully, as if something delicately poised inside me might shatter at the slightest violent movement. All at once I had a sour sense of deflation. The excitement of a moment past was gone, and there was a dull restriction in my chest, and sweat on my eyelids and my upper lip, and the damp skin under the waistband of my shorts was prickly and hot. I felt puzzled, and strangely resentful, too, as if I were the one, not she, whose private self had been intruded upon and abused. It was a manifestation of the goddess I had witnessed, no doubt of that, but the instant of divinity had been disconcertingly brief. Under my greedy gaze Mrs Grace had been transformed from woman into daemon and then in a moment was mere woman again. One moment she was Connie Grace, her husband's wife, her children's mother, the next she was an object of helpless veneration, a faceless idol, ancient and elemental, conjured by the force of my desire, and then something in her had suddenly gone slack, and I had felt a qualm of revulsion and shame, not shame for myself and what I had purloined of her but, obscurely, for the woman herself, and not for anything she had done, either, but for what she was, as with a hoarse moan she turned on her side and toppled into sleep, no longer a demon temptress but herself only, a mortal woman.

Yet for all my disconcertion it is the mortal she, and not the divine, who shines for me still, with however tarnished a gleam, amidst the shadows of what is gone. She is in my memory her own avatar. Which is the more real, the woman reclining on the grassy bank of my recollections, or the strew of dust and dried marrow that is all the earth any longer retains of her? No doubt for others elsewhere she persists, a moving figure in the waxworks of memory, but their version will be different from mine, and from each other's. Thus in the minds of the many does the one ramify and disperse. It does not last, it cannot, it is not immortality. We carry the dead with us only until we die too, and then it is we who are borne along for a little while, and then our bearers in their turn drop, and so on into the unimaginable generations. I remember Anna, our daughter Claire will remember Anna and remember me, then Claire will be gone and there will be those who remember her but not us, and that will be our final dissolution. True, there will be something of us that will remain, a fading photograph, a lock of hair, a few fingerprints, a sprinkling of atoms in the air of the room where we breathed our last, yet none of this will be us, what we are and were, but only the dust of the dead.

As a boy I was quite religious. Not devout, only compulsive. The God I venerated was Yahweh, destroyer of worlds, not gentle Jesus meek and mild. The Godhead for me was menace, and I responded with fear and its inevitable concomitant, guilt. I was a very virtuoso of guilt in those younger days, and still am in these older ones, for that matter. At the time of my First Communion, or, more to the point, the First Confession that preceded it, a priest came daily to the convent school to induct our class of fledgling penitents into the intricacies of Christian

Doctrine. He was a lean, pale fanatic with flecks of white stuff permanently at the corners of his lips. I am recalling with especial clarity an enraptured disquisition he delivered to us one fine May morning on the sin of looking. Yes, looking. We had been instructed in the various categories of sin, those of commission and omission, the mortal and the venial, the seven deadly, and the terrible ones that it was said only a bishop could absolve, but here it seemed was a new category: the passive sin. Did we imagine, Fr Foamfleck scoffingly enquired, pacing impetuously from door to window, from window to door, his cassock swishing and a star of light gleaming on his narrow, balding brow like a reflection of the divine effluvium itself, did we imagine that sin must always involve the performance of an action? Looking with lust or envy or hate is lusting, envying, hating; the wish unfollowed by the deed leaves an equal stain upon the soul. Had not the Lord himself, he cried, warming to his theme, had not the Lord himself insisted that a man who looks with an adulterous heart upon a woman has as good as committed the act? By now he had quite forgotten about us, as we sat like a little band of mice gazing up at him in awed incomprehension. Although all this was as much news to me as it was to everyone else in the class – what was adultery, a sin that only adults could commit? – I understood it well enough, in my way, and welcomed it, for even at the age of seven I was an old hand, or should I say eye, at spying upon acts I was not supposed to witness, and knew well the dark pleasure of taking things by sight and the darker shame that followed. So when I had looked my fill, and look I did and filled I was, up the silvery length of Mrs Grace's thigh to the crotch of her knickers and that crease across the plump top of her leg under her bum, it was natural that I should immediately cast about for fear that all that while someone in turn might have been looking at me, the looker. Myles who had come in from the ferns was busy ogling Rose, and Chloe was still lost in vacant reverie under the pine tree, but Mr Grace, now, had he not been observing me, all along, from under the brim of that hat of his? He sat as though collapsed into himself, his chin on his chest and his furred belly bulging out of his open shirt, a bare ankle still crossed on a bare knee, so that I could see along his inner leg, too, up to the great balled lump in his khaki shorts squeezed to bursting between thick thighs. All that long afternoon, as the pine tree spread its steadily deepening purple shadow across the grass towards him, he hardly left his folding chair except to refill his wife's wine glass or fetch something to eat – I can see him, crushing half a ham sandwich between bunched fingers and thumb and stuffing the resultant mush at one go into the red hole in his beard.

To us then, at that age, all adults were unpredictable, even slightly mad, but Carlo Grace required a particularly wary monitoring. He was given to the sudden feint, the unexpected pounce. Sitting in an armchair and seemingly lost in his newspaper, he would shoot out a hand quick as a striking snake as Chloe was passing by and catch hold of her ear or a handful of her hair and twist it vigorously and painfully, with never a word or a pause in his reading, as if arm and hand had acted of their own volition. He would break off deliberately in the midst of saying something and go still as a statue, a hand suspended, gazing blank-eyed into the nothing beyond one's nervously twitching shoulder as if attending to some dread alarm or distant tumult that only he could hear, and then suddenly would make a sham grab at one's throat and laugh hissingly through his teeth. He would engage the postman, who was halfway to being a halfwit, in earnest consultation about the prospects for the weather or the likely outcome of an upcoming football match, nodding and frowning and fingering his beard, as if what he was hearing were the purest pearls of wisdom, and then when the poor deluded fellow had gone off, whistling pridefully, he would turn to us and grin, with lifted eyebrows and pursed lips, waggling his head in soundless mirth. Although all my attention seemed to have been trained upon the others, I think now that it was from Carlo Grace I first derived the notion that I was in the presence of the gods. For all his remoteness and amused indifference, he was the one who appeared to be in command over us all, a laughing deity, the Poseidon of our summer, at whose beck our little world arranged itself obediently into its acts and portions.

Still that day of licence and illicit invitation was not done. As Mrs Grace, stretched there on the grassy bank, continued softly snoring, a torpor descended on the rest of us in that little dell, the invisible net of lassitude that falls over a company when one of its number detaches and drops away into sleep. Myles was lying on his stomach on the grass beside me but facing in the opposite direction, still eyeing Rose where she was still seated behind me on a corner of the tablecloth, oblivious, as always, of his beady regard. Chloe was still standing in the shadow of the pine tree, holding something in her hand, her face lifted, looking up intently, at a bird, perhaps, or just at the latticework of branches against the sky, and those white puffs of cloud that had begun to inch their way in from the sea. How pensive she was yet how vividly defined, with that pine cone – was it? – in her hands, her rapt gaze fixed amongst the sunshot boughs. Suddenly she was the centre of the scene, the vanishing-point upon which everything converged, suddenly it was she for whom these patterns and these shades had been arranged with such meticulous artlessness: that white cloth on the polished grass, the leaning, blue-green tree, the frilled ferns, even those little clouds, trying to seem not to move, high up in the limitless, marine sky. I glanced at Mrs Grace asleep, glanced almost with contempt. All at once she was no more than a big archaic lifeless torso, the felled effigy of some goddess no longer worshipped by the tribe and thrown out on the midden, a target for the village boys with their slingshots and their bows and arrows.

Abruptly, as if roused by the cold touch of my scorn, she sat up and cast about her with a blurred look, blinking. She peered into her wine glass and seemed surprised to find it empty. The drop of wine that had fallen on her white halter had left a pink stain, she rubbed it with a fingertip, clicking her tongue. Then she looked about at us again and cleared her throat and announced that we should all play a game of chase. Everyone stared at her, even Mr Grace. '*I'm* not chasing anyone,' Chloe said from her place under the tree's shade, and laughed, a disbelieving snort, and when her mother said she must, and called her a spoilsport, she came and stood beside her father's chair and leaned an elbow on his shoulder and narrowed her eyes at her mother, and Mr Grace, old grinning goat god, put an arm around her hips and folded her in his hairy embrace. Mrs Grace turned to me. 'You'll play, won't you?' she said. 'And Rose.'

I see the game as a series of vivid tableaux, glimpsed instants of movement all rush and colour: Rose from the waist up racing through the ferns in her red shirt, her head held high and her black hair streaming behind her; Myles, with a streak of fern-juice on his forehead like warpaint, trying to wriggle out of my grasp as I dug my claw deeper into his flesh and felt the ball of his shoulder bone grind in its socket; another fleeting image of Rose running, this time on the hard sand beyond the clearing, where she was being chased by a wildly laughing Mrs Grace, two barefoot maenads framed for a moment by the bole and branches of the pine, beyond them the dull-silver glint of the bay and the sky a deep unvarying matt blue all the way down to the horizon. Here is Mrs Grace in a clearing in the ferns crouched on one knee like a sprinter waiting for the off, who, when I surprise her, instead of fleeing, as the rules of the game say that she should, beckons to me urgently and makes me crouch at her side and puts an arm around me and draws me tight against her so that I can feel the softly giving bulge of her breast and hear her heart beating and smell her milk-and-vinegar smell. 'Ssh!' she says and puts a finger to my lips – to mine, not her own. She is trembling, ripples of suppressed laughter run through her. I have not been so close to a grown-up woman since I was a child in my mother's arms, but in place of desire now I feel only a kind of surly dread. Rose discovers the two of us crouching there, and scowls. Mrs Grace, grasping the girl's hand as if to haul herself up, instead pulls her down on top of us, and there is a melee of arms and legs and Rose's flying hair and then the three of us, leaning back on our elbows and panting, are sprawled toe to toe in a star shape amid the crushed ferns. I scramble to my feet, suddenly afraid that Mrs Grace, my suddenly former beloved, will wantonly display her lap to me again, and she puts up a hand to shade her eyes and looks at me with an impen-etrable, hard, unwarm smile. Rose too springs up, brushing at her shirt, and mutters something angrily that I do not catch and strides off into the ferns. Mrs Grace shrugs. 'Jealous,' she says, and then bids me fetch her cigarettes, for all of a sudden, she declares, she is dying for a fag.

When we returned to the grassy bank and the pine tree Chloe and her father were not there. The remains of the picnic, scattered on the white cloth, had a look of deliberateness to them, as if they had been arranged there, a message in code for us to decipher. 'That's nice,' Mrs Grace said sourly, 'they've left the clearing-up to us.' Myles emerged from the ferns again and knelt and picked a blade of grass and blew another reed note between his thumbs and waited, still and rapt as a plaster faun, the sunlight burnishing his straw-pale hair, and a moment later from far off came Chloe's answering call, a pure high whistle piercing like a needle through the waning summer day.

On the subject of observing and being observed, I must mention the long, grim gander I took at myself in the bathroom mirror this morning. Usually these days I do not dally before my reflection any longer than is necessary. There was a time when I quite liked what I saw in the looking-glass, but not any more. Now I am startled, and more than startled, by the visage that so abruptly appears there, never and not at all the one that I expect. I have been elbowed aside by a parody of myself, a sadly dishevelled figure in a Hallowe'en mask made of sagging, pinkish-grey rubber that bears no more than a passing resemblance to the image of what I look like that I stubbornly retain in my head. Also, there is the problem that I have with mirrors. That is, I have many problems with mirrors, but mostly they are metaphysical in nature, whereas the one I speak of is entirely practical. Because of my inordinate and absurd size, shaving mirrors and the like are always set too low for me on the wall, so that I have to lean down to be able to view the entirety of my face. Lately when I see myself peering out of the glass, stooped like that, with that expression of dim surprise and vague, slow fright which is perpetual with me now, mouth slack and eyebrows arched as if in weary astonishment, I feel I have definitely something of the look of a hanged man.

When I came here first I thought of growing a beard, out of inertia more than anything else, but after three or four days I noticed that the stubble was of a peculiar dark-rust colour – now I know how

Claire can be a redhead – nothing like the hair on my scalp, and frosted with specks of silver. This rufous stuff, coarse as sandpaper, combined with that shifty, bloodshot gaze, made me into a comic-strip convict, a real hard case, not yet hanged perhaps but definitely on Death Row. My temples where the greying hair has gone sparse are flecked with choco-latey, Avrilaceous freckles, or liver spots, I suppose they are, any one of which, I am all too well aware, might in a moment turn rampant at the whim of a rogue cell. I note too that my rosacea is coming on apace. The skin on my brow is marked all over with rubescent blotches and there is an angry rash on the wings of my nose, and even my cheeks are developing an unsightly red flush. My venerable and much-thumbed copy of *Black's Medical Dictionary*, by the estimable and ever unflappable William A. R. Thomson, M.D. – Adam & Charles Black, London, thirtieth edition, with 441 black-and-white, or grey-and-greyer, illustrations and four colour plates which never fail to freeze the cockles of my heart – informs me that rosacea, a nice name for an unpleasant com-plaint, is due to *a chronic congestion of the flush areas of the face and forehead, leading to the formation of red papules*; the resultant erythema, the name we medical men give to redness of the skin, tends to wax and wane but ultimately becomes permanent, *and may,* the candid Doctor warns, *be accompanied by gross enlargement of the sebaceous glands (see SKIN), leading to the gross enlargement of the nose known as rhino-phyma (qv) or grog blossoms.* The repetition there – *gross enlargement . . . gross enlargement* – is an uncharacteristic infelicity in Dr Thomson's usually euphonious if somewhat antiquated prose style. I wonder if he does house calls. He would be bound to have a calming bedside manner and a fund of information on all sorts of topics, not all of them health-related. Medical men are more versatile than they are given credit for. Roget of *Roget's Thesaurus* was a physician, did important research on consumption and laughing gas, and no doubt cured the odd patient, into the bargain. But grog blossoms, now, that is something to look forward to.

When I consider my face in the glass like this I think, naturally, of those last studies Bonnard made of himself in the bathroom mirror at Le Bosquet towards the end of the war after his wife had died – critics call these portraits pitiless, although I do not see why pity should come into it – but in fact what my reflection most reminds me of, I have just realised it, is that Van Gogh self-portrait, not the famous one with bandage and tobacco pipe and bad hat, but that one from an earlier series, done in Paris in 1887, in which he is bare-headed in a high collar and Provence-blue necktie with all ears intact, looking as if he has just emerged from some form of punitive dousing, the forehead sloped and temples concave and cheeks sunken as from hunger; he peers out from the frame sidewise, warily, with wrathful foreboding, expecting the worst, as so he should.

This morning it was the state of my eyes that struck me most forcibly, the whites all cracaleured over with those tiny bright-red veins and the moist lower lids inflamed and hanging a little way loose of the eyeballs. I have, I note, hardly any lashes left, I who when young had a silky set a girl might have envied. At the inner extremity of the upper lids there is a little bump just before the swoop of the canthus which is almost pretty except that it is permanently yellowish at the tip, as if infected. And that bud in the canthus itself, what is that for? Nothing in the human visage bears prolonged scrutiny. The pink-tinged pallor of my cheeks, which are, I am afraid, yes, sunken, just like poor Vincent's, was made the more stark and sickly by the radiance reflected off the white walls and the enamel of the sink. This radiance was not the glow of a northern autumn but seemed more like the hard, unyielding, dry glare of the far south. It glinted on the glass before me and sank into the distemper of the walls, giving them the parched, brittle texture of cuttlefish bone. A spot of it on the curve of the hand-basin streamed outward in all directions like an immensely distant nebula. Standing there in that white box of light I was transported for a moment to some far shore, real or imagined, I do not know which, although the details had a remarkable dreamlike definition, where I sat in the sun on a hard ridge of shaly sand holding in my hands a big flat smooth blue stone. The stone was dry and warm, I seemed to press it to my lips, it seemed to taste saltily of the sea's deeps and distances, far islands, lost places under leaning fronds, the frail skeletons of fishes, wrack and rot. The little waves before me at the water's edge speak with an animate voice, whispering eagerly of some ancient catastrophe, the sack of Troy, perhaps, or the sinking of Atlantis. All brims, brackish and shining. Water-beads break and fall in a silver string from the tip of an oar. I see the black ship in the distance, looming imperceptibly nearer at every instant. I am there. I hear your siren's song. I am there, almost there.

II

WE SEEMED TO SPEND, Chloe and Myles and I, the most part of our days in the sea. We swam in sunshine and in rain; we swam in the morning, when the sea was sluggish as soup, we swam at night, the water flowing over our arms like undulations of black satin; one afternoon we stayed in the water during a thunderstorm, and a fork of lightning struck the surface of the sea so close to us we heard the crackle of it and smelt the burnt air. I was not much of a swimmer. The twins had been taking lessons since they were babies and clove the waves effortlessly, like two pairs of gleaming shears. What I lacked of skill and gracefulness I made up for in stamina. I could go long distances without stopping, and frequently did, given any kind of audience, churning along steadily in sidestroke until I had exhausted not only myself but the patience of the watchers on the strand as well.

It was at the end of one of these sad little gala displays that I had my first inkling of a change in Chloe's regard for me, or, should I say, an inkling that she had a regard for me and that a change was occurring in it. Late in the evening it was, and I had swum the distance – what, a hundred, two hundred yards? – between two of the green-slimed concrete groynes that long ago had been thrown out into the sea in a vain attempt to halt the creeping erosion of the beach. I stumbled out of the waves to find that Chloe had waited for me, on the shore, all the time that I was in the water. She stood huddled in a towel, shivering in spasms; her lips were lavender. 'There's no need to show off, you know,' she said crossly. Before I could reply – and what would I have said, anyway, since she was right, I had been showing off – Myles came leaping down from the dunes above us on wheeling legs and sprayed us both with sand and at once I had an image, perfectly clear and strangely stirring, of Chloe as I had first seen her that day when she jumped from the edge of that other dune into the midst of my life. Now she handed me my towel. We three were the only ones on the beach. The misty grey air of evening had the feel of dampened ash. I see us turn and walk away towards the gap in the dunes that led to Station Road. A corner of Chloe's towel trails in the sand. I go along with my towel draped over one shoulder and my wet hair slicked down, a Roman senator in miniature. Myles runs ahead. But who is it that lingers there on the strand in the half-light, by the darkening sea that seems to arch its back like a beast as the night fast advances from the fogged horizon? What phantom version of me is it that watches us – them – those three children – as they grow indistinct in that cinereal air and then are gone through the gap that will bring them out at the foot of Station Road?

I have not yet described Chloe. In appearance there was not much difference between us, she and I, at that age, I mean in terms of what of us might have been measured. Even her hair, almost white but darkening when it was wet to the colour of polished wheat, was hardly longer than mine. She wore it in a pageboy style, with a fringe at the front overhanging her handsome, high-domed, oddly convex forehead – like, it suddenly strikes me, remarkably like the forehead of that ghostly figure seen in profile hovering at the edge of Bonnard's *Table in Front of the Window*, the one with the fruit bowl and the book and the window that itself looks like a canvas seen from behind propped on an easel; everything for me is something else, it is a thing I notice increasingly. One of the older boys from the Field assured me one day with a snicker that a fringe like Chloe's was the certain sign of a girl who played with herself. I did not know what he meant, but I felt sure that Chloe did not play, on her own or otherwise. Not for her the games of rounders or of hunt that I had formerly enjoyed with the other youngsters in the Field. And how she sneered, flaring her nostrils, when I told her that among the families in the chalets there were girls of her age who still played with dolls. She held the majority of her coevals in high scorn. No, Chloe did not play, except with Myles, and what they did together was not really play.

The boy who had remarked on her fringe – suddenly I see him, as if he were before me here, Joe somebody, a hulking, big-boned fellow with jug ears and horrent hair – also said that Chloe had green teeth. I was outraged, but he was right; there was, I saw, the next time I had the opportunity to take a close look at them, a faint tinge to the enamel of her incisors that was green indeed, but a delicate damp grey-green, like the damp light under trees after rain, or the dull-apple shade of the undersides of leaves reflected in still water. Apples, yes, her breath too had an appley smell. Little animals we were, sniffing at each other. I liked in particular, when in time I got the chance to savour it, the cheesy tang in the crevices of her elbows and her knees. She was not, I am compelled to admit, the most hygienic of girls, and in general she gave off, more strongly as the day progressed, a flattish, fawnish odour, like that which comes out of, which used to come out of, empty biscuit tins in shops – do shops still sell loose biscuits from those big square tins? Her hands. Her eyes. Her bitten fingernails. All this I remember, intensely remember, yet it is all disparate, I cannot assemble it into a unity. Try as I may, pretend as I may, I am unable to conjure her as I can her mother, say, or Myles, or even jug-eared Joe from the Field. I cannot, in short, see her. She wavers before my memory's eye at a fixed distance, always just beyond focus, moving backward at exactly the same rate as I am moving forward. But since what I am moving forward into has begun to dwindle more and more rapidly, why can I not catch up with her? Even still I sometimes see her in the street, I mean someone who might be she, with the same domed forehead and pale hair, the same headlong and yet curiously hesitant, pigeon-toed stride, but always too young, years, years too young. This is the mystery that baffled me then, and that baffles me yet. How could she be with me one moment and the next not? How could she be elsewhere, absolutely? That was what I could not understand, could not be reconciled to, cannot still. Once out of my presence she should by right become pure figment, a memory of mine, a dream of mine, but all the evidence told me that even away from me she remained solidly, stubbornly, incomprehensibly herself. And yet people do go, do vanish. That is the greater mystery; the greatest. I too could go, oh, yes, at a moment's notice I could go and be as though I had not been, except that the long habit of living indisposeth me for dying, as Doctor Browne has it.

'*Patient*,' Anna said to me one day towards the end, 'that is an odd word. I must say, I don't feel patient at all.'

When exactly I transferred my affections – how incorrigibly fond I am of these old-fashioned formulations! – from mother to daughter I cannot recollect. There was that moment of insight and intensity at the picnic, with Chloe, under the pine tree, but that was an aesthetic rather than amorous or erotic crystallisation. No, I recall no grand moment of recognition and acknowledgment, no slipping of Chloe's hand shyly into mine, no sudden stormy embrace, no stammered profession of eternal love. That is, there must have been some or even all of these, must have been a first time we held hands, embraced, made declarations, but these first times are lost in the folds of an ever more evanescent past. Even that evening when with chattering teeth I waded out of the sea and found her waiting for me blue-lipped on the strand in the dusk I did not suffer the soundless detonation that love is supposed to set off in even a boy's supposedly unsusceptible breast. I saw how cold she was, and realised how long she had waited, registered too the brusquely tender way in which she drew the wing of the towel across my scrawny, goosefleshed ribs and draped it on my shoulder, but saw and realised and registered with little more than a mild glow of gratification, as though a warm breath had fanned across a flame burning inside me somewhere in the vicinity of my heart and made it briefly flare. Yet all along a transmutation, not to say a transubstantiation, must have been taking place, in secret.

I do recall a kiss, one out of the so many that I have forgotten. Whether or not it was our first kiss I do not know. They meant so much then, kisses, they could set the whole kit and caboodle going, flares and firecrackers, fountains, gushing geysers, the lot. This one took place – no, was exchanged – no, was consummated, that is the word, in the corrugated-iron picture-house, which all along has been surreptitiously erecting itself for this very purpose out of the numerous sly references I have sprinkled through these pages. It was a barn-like structure set on a bit of scrubby waste-land between the Cliff Road and the beach. It had a steeply angled roof and no windows, only a door at the side, hung with a long curtain, of leather, I think, or somesuch stiff heavy stuff, to keep the screen from being whited-out when late-comers slipped in during matinées or at evening while the sun was shooting out its last piercing rays from behind the tennis courts. For seating there were wooden benches – we called them forms – and the screen was a large square of linen which any stray draught would set languorously asway, giving an extra undulation to some heroine's silk-clad hips or an incongruous quiver to a fearless gunslinger's gun-hand. The proprietor was a Mr Reckett, or Rickett, a small man in a Fair Isle jumper, assisted by his two big handsome teenage sons, who were a little ashamed, I always thought, of the family business, with its taint of peep-shows and the burlesque. There was only one projector, a noisy affair with a tendency to overheat – I am convinced I once saw smoke coming out of its innards – so that a full-length feature required at least two reel changes. During these intervals Mr R., who was also the projectionist, did not raise the lights, thus affording – deliberately, I am sure, for Reckett's or Rickett's Picture-House had an invitingly disreputable reputation – the numerous couples in the house, even the under-age ones, an opportunity for a minute or two of covert erotic fumbling in the pitch-dark.

On that afternoon, the rainy Saturday afternoon of this momentous kiss I am about to describe, Chloe and I were sitting in the middle of a bench near the front, so close to the screen that it seemed to tilt out over us at the top and even the most benign of the black-and-white phantoms flickering across it loomed with a manic intensity. I had been holding Chloe's hand for so long I had ceased to feel it in mine – not the primal encounter itself could have fused two fleshes so thoroughly as did those early hand-holdings – and when with a lurch and a stutter the screen went blank and her fingers twitched like fishes I twitched too. Above us the screen retained a throbbing grey penumbral glow that lasted a long moment before fading, and of which something seemed to remain even when it was gone, the ghost of a ghost. In the dark there were the usual hoots and whistles and a thunderous stamping of feet. As at a signal, under this canopy of noise, Chloe and I turned our heads simultaneously and, devout as holy drinkers, dipped our faces towards each other until our mouths met. We could see nothing, which intensified all sensations. I felt as if we were flying, without effort, dream-slowly, through the dense, powdery darkness. The clamour around us was immensely far off now, the mere rumour of a distant uproar. Chloe's lips were cool and dry. I tasted her urgent breath. When at last with a strange little whistling sigh she drew her face away from mine a shimmer passed along my spine, as if something hot inside it had suddenly liquified and run down its hollow length. Then Mr Rickett or Reckett – perhaps it was Rockett? – brought the projector to sputtering life again and the crowd subsided into more or less quiet. The screen flared white, the film clattered through its gate, and in the second before the soundtrack started up I heard the heavy rain that had been drumming on the iron roof above us suddenly cease.

Happiness was different in childhood. It was so much then a matter simply of accumulation, of taking things – new experiences, new emotions – and applying them like so many polished tiles to what would someday be the marvellously finished pavilion of the self. And incredulity, that too was a large part of being happy, I mean that euphoric inability fully to believe one's simple luck. There I was, suddenly, with a girl in my arms, figuratively, at least, doing the things that grown-ups did, holding her hand, and kissing her in the dark, and, when the picture had ended, standing aside, clearing my throat in grave politeness, to allow her to pass ahead of me under the heavy curtain and through the doorway out into the rain-washed sunlight of the summer evening. I was myself and at the same time someone else, someone completely other, completely new. As I walked behind her amid the trudging crowd in the direction of the Strand Café I touched a fingertip to my lips, the lips that had kissed hers, half expecting to find them changed in some infinitely subtle but momentous way. I expected everything to be changed, like the day itself, that had been sombre and wet and hung with big-bellied clouds when we were going into the picture-house in what had still been afternoon and now at evening was all tawny sunlight and raked shadows, the scrub grass dripping with jewels and a red sail-boat out on the bay turning its prow and setting off towards the horizon's already dusk-blue distances.

The café. In the café. In the café we.

*

It was an evening just like that, the Sunday evening when I came here to stay, after Anna had gone at last. Although it was autumn and not summer the dark-gold sunlight and the inky shadows, long and slender in the shape of felled cypresses, were the same, and there was the same sense of everything drenched and jewelled and the same ultramarine glitter on the sea. I felt inexplicably lightened; it was as if the evening, in all the drench and drip of its fallacious pathos, had temporarily taken over from me the burden of grieving. Our house, or my house, as supposedly it was now, had still not been sold, I had not yet had the heart to put it on the market, but I could not have stayed there a moment longer. After Anna's death it went hollow, became a vast echo-chamber. There was something hostile in the air, too, the growling surliness of an old hound unable to understand where its beloved mistress has gone and resentful of the master who remains. Anna would allow no one to be told of her illness. People suspected something was up, but not, until the final stages, that what was up, for her, was the game itself. Even Claire had been left to guess that her mother was dying. And now it was over, and something else had begun, for me, which was the delicate business of being the survivor.

Miss Vavasour was shyly excited by my arrival, two small round spots like dabs of pink crêpe paper glowed high on her finely wrinkled cheeks and she kept clasping her hands before her and pursing her lips to stop herself smiling. When she opened the door Colonel Blunden was there, bobbing behind her in the hallway, now at this shoulder now at that; I could see straight away he did not like the look of me. I sympathise; after all, he was cock of the walk here before I came and knocked him off his perch. Keeping a choleric glare directed at my chin, which was on his eye-level, for he is low-sized despite the ramrod spine, he pumped my hand and cleared his throat, all bluff and manly and barking comments about the weather, rather over-playing the part of the old soldier, I thought. There is something about him that is not quite right, something too shiny, too studiedly plausible. Those glossy brogues, the Harris tweed jacket with leather patches on the elbows and the cuffs, the canary-yellow waistcoat he sports at weekends, it all seems a little too good to be true. He has the glazed flawlessness of an actor who has been playing the same part for too long. I wonder if he really is an old army man. He does a good job of hiding his Belfast accent but hints of it keep escaping, like trapped wind. And anyway, why hide it, what does he fear it might tell us? Miss Vavasour confides that she has spotted him on more than one occasion slipping into church of a Sunday for early mass. A Belfast Catholic colonel? Rum; very.

In the bay of the window in the lounge, formerly the living room, a hunting table was set for tea. The room was much as I remembered it, or looked as if it was as I remembered, for memories are always eager to match themselves seamlessly to the things and places of a revisited past. The table, was that the one where Mrs Grace had stood arranging flowers that day, the day of the dog with the ball? It was laid elaborately, big silver teapot with matching strainer, best bone china, antique creamer, tongs for the sugar cubes, doilies. Miss Vavasour was in Japanese mode, her hair done up in a bun and pierced with the two big crossed pins, making me think, incongruously, of those erotic prints of the Japanese eighteenth century in which puffy, porcelain-faced matrons suffer imperturbably the gross attentions of grimacing gentlemen with outsized members and, I am always struck to notice, remarkably pliant toes.

The conversation did not flow. Miss Vavasour was nervous still and the Colonel's stomach rumbled. Late sunlight striking through a bush outside in the blustery garden dazzled our eyes and made the things on the table seem to shake and shift. I felt over-sized, clumsy, constrained, like a big delinquent child sent by its despairing parents into the country to be watched over by a pair of elderly relatives. Was it all a hideous mistake? Should I mumble some excuse and flee to a hotel for the night, or go home, even, and put up with the emptiness and the echoes? Then I reflected that I had come here precisely so that it should be a mistake, that it should be hideous, that it should be, that I should be, in Anna's word, inappropriate. 'You're mad,' Claire had said, 'you'll die of boredom down there.' It was all right for her, I retorted, she had got herself a nice new flat – *wasting no time*, I did not add. 'Then come and live with me,' she said, 'there's room enough for two.' Live with her! Room for two! But I only thanked her and said no, that I wished to be on my own. I cannot bear the way she looks at me these days, all tenderness and daughterly concern, her head held to one side in just the way that Anna used to do, one eyebrow lifted and her forehead wrinkled solicitously. I do not want solicitude. I want anger, vituperation, violence. I am like a man with an agonising toothache who despite the pain takes a vindictive pleasure in prodding the point of his tongue again and again deep into the throbbing cavity. I imagine a fist flying out of nowhere and striking me full in the face, I almost feel the thud and hear the nose-bone breaking, even the thought of it affords me a grain of sad satisfaction. After the funeral, when people came back to the house – that was awful, almost unbearable – I gripped a wine glass so hard it shattered in my fist. Gratified, I watched my own blood drip as though it were the blood of an enemy to whom I had dealt a savage slash.

'So you're in the art business, then,' the Colonel said warily. 'A lot in that, yes?'

He meant money. Miss Vavasour, pinched-lipped, frowned at him fiercely and gave her head a reproving shake. 'He only writes about it,' she said in a whisper, gulping the words as she spoke them, as if that way I would be spared hearing them.

The Colonel looked quickly from me to her and back again and dumbly nodded. He expects to get things wrong, he is inured to it. He drinks his tea with a little finger cocked. The little finger of his other hand is hooked permanently flat against the palm, it is a syndrome, not uncommon, the name of which I have forgotten; it looks painful but he says it is not. He makes curiously elegant, sweeping gestures with that hand, a conductor calling up the woodwinds or urging a fortissimo from the chorus. He has a slight tremor, too, more than once the tea cup clacked against his front teeth, which must be dentures, so white and even are they. The skin of his weatherbeaten face and the backs of his hands is wrinkled and brown and shiny, like shiny brown paper that had been used to wrap something unwrappable.

'I see,' he said, not seeing at all.

One day in 1893 Pierre Bonnard spied a girl getting off a Paris tram and, attracted by her frailty and pale prettiness, followed her to her place of work, a *pompes funèbres*, where she spent her days sewing pearls on to funeral wreaths. Thus death at the start wove its black ribbon into their lives. He quickly made her acquaintance – I suppose these things were managed with ease and aplomb in the *Belle Époque* – and shortly afterwards she left her job, and everything else in her life, and went to live with him. She told him her name was Marthe de Méligny, and that she was sixteen. In fact, although he was not to discover it until more than thirty years later when he got round to marrying her at last, her real name was Maria Boursin, and when they had met she had been not sixteen but, like Bonnard, in her middle twenties. They were to remain together, through thick and thin, or rather say, through thin and thinner, until her death nearly fifty years later. Thadée Natanson, one of Bonnard's earliest patrons, in a memoir of the painter, recalled with swift, impressionistic strokes the elfin Marthe, writing of *her wild look of a bird, her movements on tiptoe*. She was secretive, jealous, fiercely possessive, suffered from a persecution complex, and was a great and dedicated hypochondriac. In 1927 Bonnard bought a house, Le Bosquet, in the undistinguished little town of Le Cannet on the Côte d'Azur, where he lived with Marthe, bound with her in intermittently tormented seclusion, until her death fifteen years later. At Le Bosquet she developed a habit of spending long hours in the bath, and it was in her bath that Bonnard painted her, over and over, continuing the series even after she had died. The *Baignoires* are the triumphant culmination of his life's work. In the *Nude in the bath, with dog*, begun in 1941, a year before Marthe's death and not completed until 1946, she lies there, pink and mauve and gold, a goddess of the floating world, attenuated, ageless, as much dead as alive, beside her on the tiles her little brown dog, her familiar, a dachshund, I think, curled watchful on its mat or what may be a square of flaking sunlight falling from an unseen window. The narrow room that is her refuge vibrates around her, throbbing in its colours. Her feet, the left one tensed at the end of its impossibly long leg, seem to have pushed the bath out of shape and made it bulge at the left end, and beneath the bath on that side, in the same force-field, the floor is pulled out of alignment too, and seems on the point of pouring away into the corner, not like a floor at all but a moving pool of dappled water. All moves here, moves in stillness, in aqueous silence. One hears a drip, a ripple, a fluttering sigh. A rust-red patch in the water beside the bather's right shoulder might be rust, or old blood, even. Her right hand rests on her thigh, stilled in the act of supination, and I think of Anna's hands on the table that first day when we came back from seeing Mr Todd, her helpless hands with palms upturned as if to beg something from someone opposite her who was not there.

She too, my Anna, when she fell ill, took to taking extended baths in the afternoon. They soothed her, she said. Throughout the autumn and winter of that twelvemonth of her slow dying we shut ourselves away in our house by the sea, just like Bonnard and his Marthe at Le Bosquet. The weather was mild, hardly weather at all, the seemingly unbreakable summer giving way imperceptibly to a year-end of misted-over stillness that might have been any season. Anna dreaded the coming of spring, all that unbearable bustle and clamour, she said, all that life. A deep, dreamy silence accumulated around us, soft and dense, like silt. She was so quiet, there in the bathroom on the first-floor return, that I became alarmed sometimes. I imagined her slipping down without a sound in the enormous old claw-footed bath until her face was under the surface and taking a last long watery breath. I would creep down the stairs and stand on the return, not making a sound, seeming suspended there, as if I were the one under water, listening desperately through the panels of the door for sounds of life. In some foul and treacherous chamber of my heart, of course, I wanted her to have done it, wanted it all to be over with, for me as well as for her. Then I would hear a soft heave of water as she stirred, the soft splash as she lifted a hand for the soap or a towel, and I would turn away and plod back to my room and shut the door behind me and sit down at my desk and gaze out into the luminous grey of evening, trying to think of nothing.

'Look at you, poor Max,' she said to me one day, 'having to watch your words and be nice all the time.' She was in the nursing home by then, in a room at the far end of the old wing with a corner window that looked out on a wedge of handsomely unkempt lawn and a restless and, to my eye, troubling stand of great tall blackish-green trees. The spring that she had dreaded had come and gone, and she had been too ill to mind its agitations, and now it was a damply hot, glutinous summer, the last one she would see. 'What do you mean,' I said, 'having to be nice?' She said so many strange things nowadays, as if she were already somewhere else, beyond me, where even words had a different meaning. She moved her head on the pillow and smiled at me. Her face, worn almost to the bone, had taken on a frightful beauty. 'You are not even allowed to hate me a little, any more,' she said, 'like you used to.' She looked out at the trees a while and then turned back to me again and smiled again and patted my hand. 'Don't look so worried,' she said. 'I hated you, too, a little. We were human beings, after all.' By then the past tense was the only one she cared to employ.

'Would you like to see your room now?' Miss Vavasour enquired. Last spikes of sunlight through the bay window before us were falling like shards of glass in a burning building. The Colonel was brushing crossly at the front of his yellow waistcoat where he had spilled a splash of tea. He looked put-out. Probably he had been saying something to me and I had not been listening. Miss Vavasour led the way into the hall. I was nervous of this moment, the moment when I would have to take on the house, to put it on, as it were, like something I had worn in another, prelapsarian life, a once fashionable hat, say, an outmoded pair of shoes, or a wedding suit, smelling of mothballs and no longer fitting around the waist and too tight under the arms but bulging with memories in every pocket. The hall I did not recognise at all. It is short, narrow and ill-lit, and the walls are divided horizontally by a beaded runner and papered on their lower halves with painted-over anaglypta that looks to be a hundred years old or more. I do not recall there having been a hallway here. I thought the front door opened directly into — well, I am not sure what I thought it opened into. The kitchen? As I padded behind Miss Vavasour with my bag in my hand, like the well-mannered murderer in some old black-and-white thriller, I found that the model of the house in my head, try as it would to accommodate itself to the original, kept coming up against a stubborn resistance. Everything was slightly out of scale, all angles slightly out of true. The staircase was steeper, the landing pokier, the lavatory window looked not on to the road, as I thought it should, but back across the fields. I experienced a sense almost of panic as the real, the crassly complacent real, took hold of the things I thought I remembered and shook them into its own shape. Something precious was dissolving and pouring away between my fingers. Yet how easily, in the end, I let it go. The past, I mean the real past, matters less than we pretend. When Miss Vavasour left me in what from now on was to be *my room* I threw my coat over a chair and sat down on the side of the bed and breathed deep the stale unlived-in air, and felt that I had been travelling for a long time, for years, and had at last arrived at the destination to where, all along, without knowing it, I had been bound, and where I must stay, it being, for now, the only possible place, the only possible refuge, for me.

My friendly robin appeared a moment ago in the garden and I suddenly realised what it was that Avril's freckles reminded me of, that day of our encounter in Duignan's yard. The bird as usual stops on its thirdmost perch in the holly bush and studies the lay of the land with a truculent, bead-bright eye. Robins are a famously fearless breed, and this one seems quite unconcerned when Tiddles from next door comes stalking through the long grass, and even gives what sounds like a sardonic cheep and ruffles up its feathers and expands its blood-orange breast, as if to demonstrate teasingly what a plump and toothsome morsel it would make, if cats could fly. Seeing the bird alight there I remembered at once, with a pang that was exactly the same size and as singular as the bird itself, the nest in the gorse bushes that was robbed. I was quite a bird enthusiast as a boy. Not the watching kind, I was never a watcher, I had no interest in spotting and tracking and classifying, all that would have been beyond me, and would have bored me, besides; no, I could hardly distinguish one species from another, and knew little and cared less about their history or habits. I could find their nests, though, that was my specialty. It was a matter of patience, alertness, quickness of eye, and something else, a capacity to be at one with the tiny creatures I was tracking to their lairs. A savant whose name for the moment I forget has posited as a refutation of something or other the assertion that it is impossible for a human being to imagine fully what it would be like to be a bat. I take his point in general, but I believe I could have given him a fair account of such creaturehood when I was young and still part animal myself.

I was not cruel, I would not kill a bird or steal its eggs, certainly not. What drove me was curiosity, the simple passion to know something of the secrets of other, alien lives.

A thing that always struck me was the contrast between nest and egg, I mean the contingency of the former, no matter how well or even beautifully it was fashioned, and the latter's completedness, its pristine fulness. Before it is a beginning an egg is an absolute end. It is the very definition of self-containment. I hated to see a broken egg, that tiny tragedy. In the instance I am thinking of I must inadvertently have led someone to the nest. It was in a clump of gorse on a slanted headland in the midst of open fields, I would easily have been spotted going to it, as I had been doing for weeks, so that the hen bird had grown used to me. What was it, thrush, blackbird? Some such largish species, anyway. Then one day I arrived and the eggs were gone. Two had been taken and the third was smashed on the ground under the bush. All that remained of it was a smear of mingled yolk and glair and a few fragments of shell, each with its stippling of tiny, dark-brown spots. I should not make too much of the moment, I am sure I was as sentimentally heartless as the next boy, but I can still see the gorse, I can smell the buttery perfume of its blossoms, I can recall the exact shade of those brown speckles, so like the ones on Avril's pallid cheeks and on the saddle of her nose. I have carried the memory of that moment through a whole half century, as if it were the emblem of something final, precious and irretrievable.

Anna leaning sideways from the hospital bed, vomiting on to the floor, her burning brow pressed in my palm, full and frail as an ostrich egg.

I am in the Strand Café, with Chloe, after the pictures and that memorable kiss. We sat at a plastic table drinking our favourite drink, a tall glass of fizzy orange crush with a dollop of vanilla ice cream floating in it. Remarkable the clarity with which, when I concentrate, I can see us there. Really, one might almost live one's life over, if only one could make a sufficient effort of recollection. Our table was near the open doorway from which a fat slab of sunlight lay fallen at our feet. Now and then a breeze from outside would wander in absent-mindedly, strewing a whisper of fine sand across the floor, or bringing with it an empty sweet-paper that advanced and stopped and advanced again, making a scraping sound. There was hardly anyone else in the place, some boys, or young men, rather, in a corner at the back playing cards, and behind the counter the proprietor's wife, a large, sandy-haired, not unhandsome woman, gazing off through the doorway in a blank-eyed dream. She wore a pale-blue smock or apron with a scalloped white edging. What was her name? What was it. No, it will not come – so much for Memory's prodigious memory. Mrs Strand, I shall call her Mrs Strand, if she has to be called anything. She had a particular way of standing, certainly I remember that, sturdy and four-square, one freckled arm extended and a fist pressed knuckles-down on the high back of the cash-register. The ice cream and orange mixture in our glasses had a topping of sallow froth. We drank through paper straws, avoiding each other's eye in a new access of shyness. I had a sense of a general, large, soft settling, as of a sheet unfurling and falling on a bed, or a tent collapsing into the cushion of its own air. The fact of that kiss in the dark of the picture-house – I am coming to think it must have been our first kiss, after all – sat like an amazement between us, unignorably huge. Chloe had the faintest blond shadow of a moustache, I had felt its sable touch against my lip. Now my glass was almost empty and I was afraid the last of the liquid in the straw would do its embarrassing intestinal rattle. Covertly from under lowered lids I looked at Chloe's hands, one resting on the table and the other holding her glass. The fingers were fat to the first knuckle and from there tapered to the tip:

her mother's hands, I realised. Mrs Strand's wireless set was playing some song to the swoony tune of which Chloe absently hummed along. Songs were so important then, moaning of longing and loss, the very twang of what we thought was love. In the night as I lay in my bed in the chalet the melodies would come to me, a faint, brassy blaring carried on the sea breeze from the ballrooms at the Beach Hotel or the Golf, and I would think of the couples, the permed girls in brittle blues and acid greens, the quiffed young men in chunky sportscoats and shoes with inch-thick, squashy soles, circling there in the dusty, hot half-dark. *O darling lover lonesome moonlight kisses heart and soul!* And beyond all that, outside, unseen, the beach in the darkness, the sand cool on top but keeping still the day's warmth underneath, and the long lines of white waves breaking on the bias, lit from inside themselves somehow, and over everything the night, silent, secret and intent.

'That picture was stupid,' Chloe said. She brought her face close to the rim of the glass, her fringe hanging free. Her hair was pale as the sunlight on the floor at her foot . . . But wait, this is wrong. This cannot have been the day of the kiss. When we left the picture-house it was evening, an evening after rain, and now it is the middle of an afternoon, hence that soft sunlight, that meandering breeze. And where is Myles? He was with us at the pictures, so where would he have gone, he who never left his sister's side unless driven from it? Really, Madam Memory, I take back all my praise, if it is Memory herself who is at work here and not some other, more fanciful muse. Chloe gave a snort. 'As if they wouldn't have known that highwayman was a woman.'

I looked at her hands again. The one that had been holding the glass high up had slipped down to encircle the base, in which a spiked point of pure white light steadily burned, while the other, bending the straw to her lips delicately between a thumb and forefinger, cast a pale shadow on the table in the shape of a bird's beaked and high-plumed head. Again I thought of her mother, and this time I felt briefly something sharp and burning in my breast, as if a heated needle had touched my heart. Was it a twinge of guilt? For what would Mrs Grace feel, what would she say, if she were to spy me here at this table ogling the mauve shading in the hollow of her daughter's cheek as she sucked up the last of her ice-cream soda? But I did not really care, not deep down, deep past guilt and suchlike affects. Love, as we call it, has a fickle tendency to transfer itself, by a heartless, sidewise shift, from one bright object to a brighter, in the most inappropriate of circumstances. How many wedding days have ended with the tipsy and dyspeptic groom gazing miserably down on his brand-new bride bouncing under him on the king-size bed of the honeymoon suite and seeing her best friend's face, or the face of her prettier sister or even, heaven help us, of her sportive mother?

Yes, I was falling in love with Chloe – had fallen, the thing was done already. I had that sense of anxious euphoria, of happy, helpless toppling, which the one who knows he will have to do the loving always feels, at the precipitous outset. For even at such a tender age I knew that there is always a lover and a loved, and knew which one, in this case, I would be. Those weeks with Chloe were for me a series of more or less enraptured humiliations. She accepted me as a suppliant at her shrine with disconcerting complacency. In her more distracted moods she would hardly deign to notice my presence, and even when she gave me her fullest attention there was always a flaw in it, a fleck of preoccupation, of absence. This wilful vagueness tormented and infuriated me, but worse was the possibility that it might not be willed. That she might choose to disdain me I could accept, could welcome, even, in an obscurely pleasurable way, but the thought that there were intervals when I simply faded to transparency in her gaze, no, that was not to be borne. Often when I broke in on one of her vacant silences she would give a faint start and glance quickly about, at the ceiling or into a corner of the room, anywhere but at me, in search of the source of the voice that had addressed her. Was this a heartless teasing or were these moments of blankness genuine? Galled beyond bearing I would seize her by the shoulders and shake her, demanding that she see me and only me, but she would go slack in my hands and cross her eyes and let her head waggle like a rag doll's, laughing in her throat and sounding unnervingly like Myles, and when I flung her roughly from me in disgust she would fall back on sand or sofa and lie sprawled with limbs awry and pretend to be grotesquely, grinningly, dead.

Why did I put up with her caprices, her high-handedness? I was never one to suffer slights easily, and always made sure to get my own back, even on loved ones, or on loved ones especially. My forbearance in Chloe's case was due, I believe, to a strong urge of protectiveness that I had towards her. Let me explain, it is interesting, I think it is interesting. A nice, an exquisite, tactfulness was in operation here.

Since she was the one on whom I had chosen, or had been chosen, to lavish my love, she must be preserved as nearly flawless as possible, spiritually and in her actions. It was imperative that I save her from herself and her faults. The task fell to me naturally since her faults were her faults, and she could not be expected to evade their bad effects by her own volition. And not only must she be saved from these faults and their consequences for her behaviour but she must be kept from all knowledge of them, too, insofar as it was possible for me to do so. And not just her active faults. Ignorance, incapacity of insight, dull complacency, such things too must be masked, their manifestations denied. The fact for instance that she did not know that she was later in my affections than her mother, of all people, made her seem almost piteously vulnerable in my eyes. Mark, the issue was not the fact of her being a late-comer in my affections, but her ignorance of that fact. If she were somehow to find out my secret she would likely be let down in her own estimation, would think herself a fool not to have seen what I felt for her mother, and might even be tempted to feel second to her mother in having been my second choice. And that must not be.

In case I should seem to be casting myself in too benevolent a light, I hasten to say that my concern and care in the matter of Chloe and her shortcomings was not for her benefit alone. Her self-esteem was of far less importance to me than my own, although the latter was dependent on the former. If her sense of herself were tainted, by doubt or feelings of foolishness or of lack of perspicacity, my regard for her would itself be tainted. So there must be no confrontations, no brutal enlightenments, no telling of terrible truths. I might shake her by the shoulders until her bones rattled, I might throw her to the ground in disgust, but I must not tell her that I had loved her mother before I loved her, that she smelled of stale biscuits, or that Joe from the Field had remarked the green tinge of her teeth. As I walked meekly behind her swaggering figure, my fond and fondly anguished gaze fixed on the blond comma of hair at the nape of her neck or the hairline cracks in the porcelain backs of her knees, I felt as if I were carrying within me a phial of the most precious and delicately combustible material. No, no sudden movements, none at all.

There was another reason why she must be kept inviolate, unpolluted by too much self-knowledge or, indeed, too sharp a knowledge of me. This was her *difference*. In her I had my first experience of the absolute otherness of other people. It is not too much to say — well, it is, but I shall say it anyway — that in

Chloe the world was first manifest for me as an objective entity. Not my father and mother, my teachers, other children, not Connie Grace herself, no one had yet been real in the way that Chloe was. And if she was real, so, suddenly, was I. She was I believe the true origin in me of self-consciousness. Before, there had been one thing and I was part of it, now there was me and all that was not me. But here too there is a torsion, a kink of complexity. In severing me from the world and making me realise myself in being thus severed, she expelled me from that sense of the immanence of all things, the all things that had included me, in which up to then I had dwelt, in more or less blissful ignorance. Before, I had been housed, now I was in the open, in the clearing, with no shelter in sight. I did not know that I would not get inside again, through that ever straitening gate.

I never knew where I was with her, or what sort of treatment to expect at her hands, and this was, I suspect, a large part of her attraction for me, such is the quixotic nature of love. One day when we were walking along the beach at the water's edge searching after a particular kind of pink shell she needed to make a necklace she stopped suddenly and turned and, ignoring the bathers in the water and the picnickers on the sand, seized me by the shirt-front and pulled me to her and kissed me with such force that my upper lip was crushed against my front teeth and I tasted blood, and Myles, behind us, did his throaty chuckle. In a moment she had pushed me away, in high disdain, it seemed, and was walking on, frowning, her eye as before moving sharply along the waterline where the bland, packed sand greedily inhaled the outrun of each encroaching wave with a sucking sigh. I looked about anxiously. What if my mother had been there to see, or Mrs Grace, or Rose, even? But Chloe seemed not to care. I can still recall the grainy sensation as the soft pulp of our lips was ground between our teeth.

She liked to throw down dares, but was vexed when they were taken up. Early one eerily still morning, with thunder clouds on the far horizon and the sea flat and greyly lucent, I was standing before her waist-deep in the warmish wash and about to dive and swim between her legs, if she would let me, which she sometimes did. 'Go on, quick,' she said, narrowing her eyes, 'I've just done a pee.' I could not but do as she urged, aspiring little gentleman that I was. But when I surfaced again she said I was disgusting, and leaned into the water to her chin and swam slowly away.

She was prone to sudden and unnerving flashes of violence. I am thinking of one wet afternoon when we were alone together in the living room at the Cedars. The air in the room was damply chill and there was the sad, rainy-day smell of soot and cretonne curtains. Chloe had come in from the kitchen and was crossing to the window and I stood up from the sofa and went towards her, I suppose to try to get my arms around her. Immediately at my approach she stopped and brought up her hand in a quick short arc and delivered me a slap full in the face. So sudden was the blow, so complete, it seemed a definition of some small, unique and vital thing. I heard the echo of it ping back from a corner of the ceiling. We stood a moment motionless, I with my face averted, and she took a step backward, and laughed, and then pouted sulkily and went on to the window, where she picked up something from the table and looked at it with a fierce frown.

There was a day on the beach when she fixed on a townie to torment. It was a blustery grey afternoon towards the end of the holiday, the faintest of autumnal notes already in the air, and she was bored and in malevolent mood. The townie was a pale, shivering fellow in sagging black swimming trunks, with a concave chest and nipples swollen and discoloured from the cold. We cornered him, the three of us, behind a concrete groyne. He was taller than the twins, but I was taller still, and being eager to impress my girl I gave him a good hard push and knocked him back against the green-slimed wall, and Chloe planted herself in front of him and at her most imperious demanded to know his name and what he was doing here. He looked at her in slow bewilderment, unable to understand, it seemed, why he had been picked on, or what it was we wanted of him, which of course we did not know either. 'Well?' Chloe cried, hands on her hips and tapping one foot on the sand. He smiled uncertainly, more embarrassed than in fear of her. He had come down for the day, he said, mumbling, with his Mammy, on the train. 'Oh, your Mammy, is it?' Chloe said with a sneer, and as if that were a signal Myles stepped forward and smacked him hard on the side of the head with the flat of his hand, producing an impressively loud sharp *tock!* 'See?' Chloe said shrilly. 'That's what you get for being smart with us!' The townie, poor slow sheep that he was, only looked startled, and put up a hand and felt his face as if to verify the amazing fact of having been hit. There was a thrilling moment of stillness then when anything might have happened. Nothing did. The townie only gave a sort of resigned, sad shrug and shambled away, still with a hand lifted to his jaw, and Chloe turned on me defiantly but said nothing, while Myles only laughed.

What remained with me from the incident was not Chloe's glare or Myles's snigger, but the look the townie gave me at the end, before turning disconsolately away. He knew me, knew I was a townie too, like him, whatever I might try to seem. If in that look there had been an accusation of betrayal, of anger at me for siding with strangers against him, anything like that, I would not have minded, but would, in fact, have felt gratified, even if shamefacedly so. No, what unsettled me was the expression of acceptance in his glance, the ovine unsurprisedness at my perfidy. I had an urge to hurry after him and put a hand on his shoulder, not so that I might apologise or try to excuse myself for helping to humiliate him, but to make him look at me again, or, rather, to make him withdraw that other look, to negate it, to wipe the record of it from his eye. For I found intolerable the thought of being known in the way that he seemed to know me. Better than I knew myself. Worse.

I have always disliked being photographed, but I intensely disliked being photographed by Anna. It is a strange thing to say, I know, but when she was behind a camera she was like a blind person, something in her eyes went dead, an essential light was extinguished. She seemed not to be looking through the lens, at her subject, but rather to be peering inward, into herself, in search of some defining perspective, some essential point of view. She would hold the camera steady at eye-level and thrust her raptor's head out sideways and stare for a second, sightlessly, it might be, as if one's features were written in some form of braille that she was capable of reading at a distance; when she pressed the shutter it seemed the least important thing, no more than a gesture to placate the apparatus. In our early days together I was unwise enough to allow her to persuade me to pose for her on a few occasions; the results were shockingly raw, shockingly revealing. In those half-dozen black-and-white head-and-shoulders shots that she took of me – and took is the word – I seemed to myself more starkly on show than I would have been in a full-length study and wearing not a stitch. I was young and smooth and not unhandsome – I am being modest – but in those photographs I appeared an overgrown homunculus. It was not that she made me look ugly or deformed. People who saw the photographs said they flattered me. I was not flattered, far from it. In them I appeared to have been grabbed and held for an instant on the point of fleeing, with cries of *Stop, thief!* ringing about me. My expression was uniformly winsome and ingratiating, the expression of a miscreant who fears he is about to be accused of a crime he knows he has committed yet cannot quite recall, but is preparing his extenuations and justifications anyway. What a desperate, beseeching smile I wore, a leer, a very leer. She trained her camera on a fresh-faced hopeful but the pictures she produced were the mug-shots of a raddled old confidence trickster. Exposed, yes, that is the word, too.

It was her special gift, the disenchanted, disenchanting, eye. I am thinking of the photographs she took in the hospital, at the end, at the beginning of the end, when she was still undergoing treatment and had strength enough to get up from her bed unaided. She had Claire search out her camera, it was years since she had used it. The prospect of this return to an old obsession gave me a strong yet unaccountable sense of foreboding. I found disturbing too, although again I could not have said exactly why, the fact that it was Claire, and not I, whom she had asked to fetch the camera, and in the tacit understanding, furthermore, that I was not to hear of it. What did it mean, all this secrecy and hugger-mugger? Claire, lately returned briefly from her studies abroad – France, the Low Countries, Vaublin, all that – was shocked to find her mother so ill, and was angry at me, of course, for not summoning her sooner. I did not tell her that Anna was the one who had not wanted her home. This too was odd, for in the past they had always been close, that pair. Was I jealous? Yes, a little, in fact more than a little, if I am to be honest. I am well aware of what I expected, what I expect, of my daughter, and of the selfishness and pathos of that expectation. Much is demanded of the dilettante's off-spring. She will do what I could not, and be a great scholar, if I have any say in the matter, and I have. Her mother left her some money, but not enough. I am the big fat goose, and costive with the golden eggs.

It was by chance that I caught Claire smuggling the camera out of the house. She tried to pass it off casually, but Claire is not good at being casual. Not that she knew, any more than I did, why it should be a secret. Anna always had an underhand way of going about the simplest things, it was the lingering influ-ence of her father and their rackety early life together, I suppose. There was a childish side to her. I mean she was wilful, secretive, and deeply resentful of the slightest interference or objection. I can talk, I know. I think it must be that we were both only children.

That sounds odd. I mean that we were both the only children of our parents. That sounds odd too. Did I seem to disapprove of her attempts to be an artist, if taking snapshots can be considered artistry? In fact, I paid scant attention to her photographs, and she had no reason to think I would have kept the camera from her. It is all very puzzling.

Anyway, a day or two after I caught Claire with the camera I was called in by the hospital to be sternly informed that my wife had been taking photographs of the other patients and that there had been complaints. I blushed on Anna's behalf, standing in front of the Matron's desk and feeling like a schoolboy hauled up before the Head to account for someone else's misdeeds. It seemed Anna had been wandering through the wards, barefoot, in her hospital-issue bleached white smock, wheeling her drip-feed stand – she called it her dumb-waiter – in search of the more grievously marked and maimed among her fellow patients, by whose bedsides she would park the drip stand and bring out her Leica and snap away until she was spotted by one or other of the nurses and ordered back to her room.

'Did they tell you who complained?' she demanded of me sulkily. 'Not the patients, only the relatives, and what do they know?'

She had me bring the film for developing to her friend Serge. Her friend Serge, who at one time in the far past may possibly have been more than a friend, is a burly fellow with a limp and a mane of beautiful black hair which he tosses back from his forehead with a graceful sweep of both his big blunt hands. He has a studio at the top of one of those tall narrow old houses in Shade Street, by the river. He takes fashion photographs, and sleeps with his models. He claims to be a refugee from somewhere or other, and speaks with a lisping accent which the girls are said to find irresistible. He does not use a surname, and even Serge, for all I know, may be a *nom d'appareil*. He is the kind of person we used to know, Anna and I, in the old days, which were still new then. I cannot think now how I tolerated him; nothing like disaster for showing up the cheapness and fraudulence of one's world, one's former world.

There seems to be something about me that Serge finds irresistibly funny. He keeps up a stream of unamusing little jokes, which I am convinced are a pretext for him to laugh without seeming to be laughing at me. When I came to collect the developed prints he set off on a search for them amidst the picturesque disorder of the studio – it would not surprise me if he arranges the disorder, like a window display – picking his way about nimbly on his disproportionately dainty feet despite a violent list to the left at every other step. He slurped coffee from a seemingly bottomless mug and talked to me over his shoulder. The coffee is another of his trademarks, along with the hair and the limp and the Tolstoyan baggy white shirts that he favours. 'How is the beautiful Annie?' he asked. He glanced at me sidelong and laughed. He always called her Annie, which no one else did; I suppress the thought that it might have been his old love name for her. I had not told him of her illness – why should I? He was scrabbling about in the chaos on the big table he uses as a work desk. The vinegary stink of developing fluid from the darkroom was stinging my nostrils and my eyes. '*Any news of Annie,*' he warbled to himself, making a jingle of it, and gave another snuffly laugh down his nostrils. I saw myself run forward with a cry and hustle him to the window and heave him headlong down into the cobbled street. He gave a grunt of triumph and came up with a thick manila envelope, but when I reached out to take it he held back, considering me with a merrily speculative eye, his head cocked to the side. 'These things she is taking, they are some pictures,' he said, hefting the envelope in one hand and flapping the other limply up and down in his studied Mitteleuropean way. Through a skylight above us the sun of summer shone full on the work table, making the strewn sheets of photographic paper burn with a hot white glare. Serge shook his head and whistled soundlessly through pursed lips. 'Some pictures!'

From her hospital bed Anna reached up eagerly with fingers childishly splayed and snatched the envelope from my hands without a word. It was over-warm and humid in the room and there was a glistening grey film of sweat on her forehead and her upper lip. Her hair had begun to grow again, in a half-hearted fashion, as if it knew it would not be needed for long; it came out in patches, lank and black and greasy-seeming, like a cat's licked fur. I sat on the side of the bed and watched her tear impatiently with her fingernails at the flap of the envelope. What is it about hospital rooms that makes them so seductive, despite all that goes on in them? They are not like hotel rooms. Hotel rooms, even the grandest of them, are anonymous; there is nothing in them that cares for a guest, not the bed, not the refrigerated drinks cabinet, not even the trouser-press, standing so deferentially at attention with its back to the wall. Despite all efforts of architects, designers, managements, hotel rooms are always impatient for us to be gone; hospital rooms, on the contrary, and without anybody's effort, are there to make us stay, to want to stay, and be content. They have a soothing suggestion of the nursery, all that thick cream paint on the walls, the rubberised floors, the miniature hand-basin in the corner with its demure little towel on a rail underneath, and the bed, of course, with its wheels and levers, that looks like a kiddie's complicated cot, where one might sleep and dream, and be watched over, and cared for, and never, not ever, die. I wonder if I could rent one, a hospital room, that is, and work there, live there, even. The amenities would be wonderful. There would be the cheery wake-up call in the mornings, meals served with iron regularity, one's bed made up neat and tight as a long white envelope, and a whole medical team standing by to cope with any emergency. Yes, I could be content there, in one of those white cells, my barred window, no, not barred, I am getting carried away, my window looking down on the city, the smokestacks, the busy roads, the hunched houses, and all the little figures, hurrying endlessly, to and fro.

Anna spread the photographs around her on the bed and pored over them avidly, her eyes alight, those eyes that by then had come to seem enormous, starting from the armature of the skull. The first surprise was that she had used colour film, for she had always favoured black-and-white. Then there were the photographs themselves. They might have been taken in a field hospital in wartime, or in a casualty ward in a defeated and devastated city. There was an old man with one leg gone below the knee, a thick line of sutures like the prototype of a zip fastener traversing the shiny stump. An obese, middle-aged woman was missing a breast, the flesh where it had been recently removed all puckered and swollen like a giant, empty eye-socket. A big-bosomed, smiling mother in a lacy nightdress displayed a hydrocephalic baby with a bewildered look in its otter's bulging eye. The arthritic fingers of an old woman taken in close-up were knotted and knobbed like clusters of root ginger. A boy with a canker embossed on his cheek, intricate as a mandala, grinned into the camera, his two fists lifted and giving a double thumbs-up sign, a fat tongue cheekily stuck out. There was a shot angled down into a metal bin with gobs and strings of unidentifiable dark wet meat thrown into it – was that refuse from the kitchen, or the operating theatre?

What was most striking to me about the people pictured was the calmly smiling way in which they displayed their wounds, their stitches, their suppurations.

I recall in particular a large and at first sight formal study, in hard-edged shades of plastic pinks and puces and glossy greys, taken from low down at the foot of her bed, of a fat old wild-haired woman with her slack, blue-veined legs lifted and knees splayed, showing off what I presumed was a prolapsed womb. The arrangement was as striking and as carefully composed as a frontispiece from one of Blake's prophetic books. The central space, an inverted triangle bounded on two sides by the woman's cocked legs and along the top by the hem of her white gown stretched tight across from knee to knee, might have been a blank patch of parchment in wait of a fiery inscription, heralding perhaps the mock-birth of the pink and darkly purple thing already protruding from her lap. Above this triangle the woman's Medusa-head seemed by a subtle trick of perspective to have been severed and lifted forward and set down squarely in the same plane as her knees, the clean-cut stump of the neck appearing to be balanced on the straight line of the gown's hem that formed the upturned base of the triangle. Despite the position in which it found itself the face was perfectly at ease, and might even have been smiling, in a humorously deprecating fashion, with a certain satisfaction and, yes, a certain definite pride. I recalled walking in the street with

Anna one day after all her hair had fallen out and she spotted passing by on the opposite pavement a woman who was also bald. I do not know if Anna caught me catching the look they exchanged, the two of them, blank-eyed and at the same time sharp, sly, complicit. In all that endless twelvemonth of her illness I do not think I ever felt more distant from her than I did at that moment, elbowed aside by the sorority of the afflicted.

'Well?' she said now, keeping her eyes on the pictures and not bothering to look at me. 'What do you think?'

She did not care what I thought. By now she had gone beyond me and my opinions.

'Will you show them to Claire?' I asked. Why was that the first thing that came into my head?

She pretended not to have heard, or perhaps had not been listening. A bell was buzzing somewhere in the building, like a small insistent pain made audible.

'They are my dossier,' she said. 'My indictment.'

'Your indictment?' I said helplessly, feeling an obscure panic. 'Of what?'

She shrugged.

'Oh, everything,' she said, mildly. 'Everything.'

*

Chloe, her cruelty. The beach. The midnight swim. Her lost sandal, that night in the doorway of the dancehall, Cinderella's shoe. All gone. All lost. It is no matter. Tired, tired and drunk. No matter.

We have had a storm. It went on all night long and into the middle of the morning, an extraordinary affair, I have never known the like, in these temperate zones, for violence or duration. I enjoyed it outrageously, sitting up in my ornate bed as on a catafalque, if that is the word I want, the room aflicker around me and the sky stamping up and down in a fury, breaking its bones. At last, I thought, at last the elements have achieved a pitch of magnificence to match my inner turmoil! I felt transfigured, I felt like one of Wagner's demi-gods, aloft on a thunder-cloud and directing the great booming chords, the clashes of celestial cymbals. In this mood of histrionic euphoria, fizzing with brandy-fumes and static, I considered my position in a new and crepitant light. I mean my general position. I have ever had the conviction, resistant to all rational considerations, that at some unspecified future moment the continuous rehearsal which is my life, with its so many misreadings, its slips and fluffs, will be done with and that the real drama for which I have ever and with such earnestness been preparing will at last begin. It is a common delusion, I know, everyone entertains it. Yet last night, in the midst of that spectacular display of Valhallan petulance, I wondered if the moment of my entrance might be imminent, the moment of my *going on*, so to say. I do not know how it would be, this dramatic leap into the thick of the action, or what exactly might be expected to take place, onstage. Yet I anticipate an apotheosis of some kind, some grand climacteric. I am not speaking here of a posthumous transfiguration. I do not entertain the possibility of an afterlife, or any deity capable of offering it. Given the world that he created, it would be an impiety against God to believe in him. No, what I am looking forward to is a moment of earthly expression. That is it, that is it exactly: I shall be expressed, totally. I shall be delivered, like a noble closing speech. I shall be, in a word, *said*. Has this not always been my aim, is this not, indeed, the secret aim of all of us, to be no longer flesh but transformed utterly into the gossamer of unsuffering spirit? Bang, crash, shudder, the very walls shaking.

By the way: the bed, my bed. Miss Vavasour insists it has always been here. The Graces, mother and father, was it theirs, is this where they slept, in this very bed? What a thought, I do not know what to do with it. Stop thinking it, that would be best; least unsettling, that is.

Another week done with. How quickly the time goes as the season advances, the earth hurtling along its groove into the year's sharply descending final arc. Despite the continuing clemency of the weather the Colonel feels the winter coming on. He has been unwell of late, has caught what he says is a cold on the kidneys. I tell him that was one of my mother's complaints – *one of her favourites, in fact*, I do not add – but he gives me a queer look, thinking I am mocking him, perhaps, as perhaps I am. What is a cold on the kidneys, anyway? Ma was no more specific than the Colonel on the subject, and even *Black's Medical* can offer no enlightenment. Maybe he wants me to think this is the reason for his frequent shufflings to the lavatory by day and night and not the something more serious that I suspect. 'I'm not the best,' he says, 'and that's a fact.' He has taken to wearing a muffler at mealtimes. He turns over his food listlessly and greets the mildest attempt at levity with a soulful, suffering glance that drops wearily away to the accompaniment of a faint sigh that is almost a moan. Have I described his fascinatingly chromatic nose? It changes hue with the time of day and the slightest variation of the weather, from pale lavender through burgundy to the deepest imperial purple. Is this rhinophyma, I suddenly wonder, are these Dr Thomson's famous grog blossoms? Miss Vavasour is sceptical of his complaints, and makes a wry face at me when he is not looking. I think he is losing heart in his attempts to woo her. In that bright-yellow waistcoat, the bottom button always punctiliously undone and the pointed flaps open over his neat little paunch, he is as intent and circumspect as one of those outlandishly plumed male birds, peacock or cock pheasant, who gorgeously stalk up and down at a distance, desperate of eye but pretending indifference, while the drab hen unconcernedly pecks in the gravel for grubs. Miss V. bats aside his ponderously coy attentions with a mixture of vexation and flustered embarrassment. I surmise, from the injured looks he throws at her, that previously she gave him some grounds for hope which were immediately whipped from under him when I came along to be a witness to her folly, and that now she is cross at herself and eager I should be convinced that what he may have taken for encouragement was really no more than a display of a landlady's professional politesse.

Often at a loss myself to know what to do with my time, I have been compiling a schedule of the Colonel's typical day. He rises early, for he is a poor sleeper, suggesting to us by expressive silences and tight-lipped shrugs a fund of battleground nightmares that would keep a narcolept from sleep, although I have an idea the bad memories that beset him were gathered not in the far-flung colonies but somewhere nearer home, for example on the boreens and cratered side roads of South Armagh. Breakfast he takes alone, at a small table in the ingle-nook in the kitchen – no, I did not recall an ingle, not to speak of a nook – solitude being the preferred mode in which to partake of what he frequently and portentously pronounces *the most important meal of the day*. Miss Vavasour is content not to disturb him, and serves him his rashers and eggs and black pudding in a sardonic silence. He keeps his own supply of condiments, unlabelled bottles of brown and red and dark-green sluggish stuffs, which he doles on to his food with an alchemist's niceness of measurement. There is a spread too that he prepares himself, he calls it slap, a khaki-coloured goo involving anchovies, curry powder, a great deal of pepper, and other, unnamed things; it smells, curiously, of dog. 'A great scourer for the bag,' he says. It took me a while to realise that this bag of which he often speaks, though never in Miss V.'s presence, is the stomach and environs. He is ever alive to the state of the bag.

After breakfast comes the morning constitutional, taken in all weathers down Station Road and along the Cliff Walk past the Pier Head Bar and back again the long way round by the lighthouse cottages and the Gem, where he stops to buy the morning paper and a roll of the extra-strong peppermints which he sucks on all day, and the faint sickly smell of which pervades the house. He goes along at a brisk clip with what I am sure he intends to be a military bearing, although the first morning I saw him setting off I noted with a jolt how at every step he swings out his left foot in a tight sideways curve, exactly as my long-lost father used to do. For the first week or two of my stay here he would still bring back from these route marches a token for Miss Vavasour, nothing fancy, nothing cissyish, a spray of russet leaves or a sprig of greenery, nothing that could not be presented as merely an item of horticultural interest, which he would place without remark on the hall table beside her gardening gloves and her big bunch of house keys. Now he returns empty-handed, save for his paper and his peppermints. That is my doing; my arrival put paid to the ceremony of the nosegays.

The newspaper consumes what is left of his morning, he reads it from first page to last, gathering intelligence, missing nothing. He sits by the fireplace in the lounge, where the clock on the mantelpiece has a hesitant, geriatric tick and pauses at the half-hour and the two quarter-hours to deliver itself of a single, infirm, jangling chime but on the hour itself maintains what seems a vindictive silence. He has his armchair, his glass ashtray for his pipe, his box of Swan Vestas, his footstool, his paper rack. Does he notice those brassy beams of sunlight falling through the leaded panes of the bay window, the desiccated bunch of sea-blue and tenderly blood-brown hydrangea occupying the grate where even yet the first fire of the season has not needed to be lit? Does he notice that the world he reads about in the paper is no longer the world he knew? Perhaps these days all his energies, like mine, go into the effort of not noticing. I have caught him furtively crossing himself when the tolling of the angelus bell comes up to us from the stone church down on Strand Road.

At lunchtime the Colonel and I must shift for ourselves, for Miss Vavasour retires to her room every day between noon and three, to sleep, or read, or work on her memoirs, nothing would surprise me. The Colonel is a ruminant. He sits at the kitchen table in shirt-sleeves and an antique sleeveless pullover munching away at an ill-made sandwich – hacked lump of cheese or chunk of cold meat between two door-stoppers smeared with his slap, or a daub of Colman's fieriest, or sometimes both if he feels in need of a jolt – and tries out feints of conversation on me, like a canny field commander searching for a bulge in the enemy's defences. He sticks to neutral topics, the weather, sporting fixtures, horse racing although he assures me he is not a betting man. Despite the diffidence his need is patent: he dreads the afternoons, those empty hours, as I dread the sleepless nights. He cannot make me out, would like to know what really I am doing here, who might be anywhere, if I chose, so he believes. Who that could afford the warm south – 'The sun's the only man for the pains and aches,' the Colonel opines – would come to do his grieving at the Cedars? I have not told him about the old days here, the Graces, all that. Not that all that is an explanation. I get up to leave – 'Work,' I say solemnly – and he gives me a desperate look. Even my unforthcoming company is preferable to his room and the radio.

A chance mention of my daughter provoked an excited response. He has a daughter too, married, with a pair of little ones, as he says. They are going to come for a visit any day now, the daughter, her husband the engineer, and the girls, who are seven and three. I have a premonition of photographs and sure enough the wallet comes out of a back pocket and the snaps are shown, a leathery young woman with a dissatisfied mien who looks not at all like the Colonel, and a little girl in a party frock who misfortunately does. The son-in-law, grinning on a beach with babe in arms, is unexpectedly good-looking, a big-shouldered southern type with an oiled quiff and bruised eyes – how did mousey Miss Blunden get herself such a he-man? Other lives, other lives. Suddenly somehow they are too much for me, the Colonel's daughter, her man, their girls, and I return the pictures hastily, shaking my head. 'Oh, sorry, sorry,' the Colonel says, harrumphing embarrassedly. He thinks that talk of family stirs painful associations for me, but it is not that, or not only that. These days I must take the world in small and carefully measured doses, it is a sort of homeopathic cure I am undergoing, though I am not certain what this cure is meant to mend. Perhaps I am learning to live amongst the living again. Practising, I mean. But no, that is not it. Being here is just a way of not being anywhere.

Miss Vavasour, so assiduous in other areas of her

care of us, is capricious, not to say cavalier, in the matter not only of luncheon but of meals in general, and dinner especially at the Cedars can be an unpredictable refection. Anything might appear on the table, and does. Tonight for instance she served us breakfast kippers with poached eggs and boiled cabbage. The Colonel, sniffing, ostentatiously wielded his condiment bottles turn and turn about like a spot-the-pea artist. To these wordless protests of his Miss Vavasour's response is invariably one of aristocratic absent-mindedness verging on disdain. After the kippers there were tinned pears lodged in a gritty grey lukewarm substance which if childhood memory serves I think was semolina. Semolina, my goodness. As we made our way through this stodge, with nothing but the clicking of cutlery to disturb the silence, I had a sudden image of myself as a sort of large dark simian something slumped there at the table, or not a something but a nothing, rather, a hole in the room, a palpable absence, a darkness visible. It was very strange. I saw the scene as if from outside myself, the dining room half lit by two standard lamps, the ugly table with the whorled legs, Miss Vavasour absently at gaze and the Colonel stooped over his plate and baring one side of his upper dentures as he chewed, and I this big dark indistinct shape, like the shape that no one at the séance sees until the daguerreotype is developed. I think I am becoming my own ghost.

After dinner Miss Vavasour clears the table in a few broad fanciful passes – she is altogether too good for this kind of menial chore – while the Colonel and I sit in vague distress listening to our systems doing their best to deal with the insults with which they have just been served. Then Miss V. in stately fashion leads the way to the television room. This is a cheerless, ill-lit chamber which has a somehow subterranean atmosphere, and is always dank and cold. The furnishings too have an underground look to them, like things that subsided here over the years from some brighter place above. A chintz-covered sofa sprawls as if aghast, its two arms flung wide and cushions sagging. There is an armchair upholstered in plaid, and a small, three-legged table with a dusty potted plant which I believe is a genuine aspidistra, the like of which I have not seen since I do not know when, if ever. Miss Vavasour's upright piano, its lid shut, stands against the back wall as if in tight-lipped resentment of its gaudy rival opposite, a mighty, gunmetal-grey Pixilate Panoramic which its owner regards with a mixture of pride and slightly shamed misgiving. On this set we watch the comedy shows, favouring the gentler ones repeated from twenty or thirty years ago. We sit in silence, the canned audiences doing our laughing for us. The jittering coloured light from the screen plays over our faces. We are rapt, as mindless as children. Tonight there was a programme on a place in Africa, the Serengeti Plain, I think it was, and its great elephant herds. What amazing beasts they are, a direct link surely to a time long before our time, when behemoths even bigger than they roared and rampaged through forest and swamp. In manner they are melancholy and yet seem covertly amused, at us, apparently. They lumber along placidly in single file, the trunk-tip of one daintily furled around the laughable piggy tail of its cousin in front. The young, hairier than their elders, trot contentedly between their mothers' legs. If one set out to seek among our fellow-creatures, the land-bound ones, at least, for our very opposite, one would surely need look no further than the elephants. How is it we have allowed them to survive so long? Those sad little knowing eyes seem to invite one to pick up a blunderbuss. Yes, put a big bullet through there, or into one of those huge absurd flappy ears. Yes, yes, exterminate all the brutes, lop away at the tree of life until only the stump is left standing, then lovingly take the cleaver to that, too. Finish it all off.

You cunt, you fucking cunt, how could you go and leave me like this, floundering in my own foulness, with no one to save me from myself. *How could you.*

Speaking of the television room, I realise suddenly, I cannot think why it did not strike me before now, so obvious is it, that what it reminds me of, what the whole house reminds me of, for that matter, and this must be the real reason I came here to hide in the first place, is the rented rooms my mother and I inhabited, were forced to inhabit, throughout my teenage years. After my father left she was compelled to find work to support us and pay for my education, such as it was. We moved to the city, she and I, where she thought there would surely be more opportunities for her. She had no skills, had left school early and worked briefly as a shop-girl before she met my father and married him to get away from her family, nevertheless she was convinced that somewhere there awaited her the ideal position, the job of jobs, the one that she and only she was meant to fill but maddeningly could never find. So we shifted from place to place, from lodging house to lodging house, arriving at a new one always it seemed on a drizzly Sunday evening in winter. They were all alike, those rooms, or are so at least in my memory of them. There was the armchair with the broken arm, the pock-marked lino on the floor, the squat black gas stove sullen in its corner and smelling of the previous lodger's fried dinners. The lavatory was down the hall, with a chipped wooden seat and a long brown rust-stain on the back of the bowl and the ring-pull missing from the chain. The smell in the hall was like the smell of my breath when I breathed and rebreathed it into my cupped hands to know what it would be like to be suffocated. The surface of the table we ate at had a tacky feel under the fingers no matter how hard she scrubbed at it. After our tea she would clear away the tea things and spread out the *Evening Mail* on the table under the wan glow of a sixty-watt bulb and run a hairpin down the columns of job ads, ticking off each ad and muttering angrily under her breath. '*Previous experience essential . . . references required . . . must be university graduate . . .* Huh!' Then the greasy pack of cards, the matches divided into two equal piles, the tin ashtray overflowing with her cigarette butts, the cocoa for me and the glass of cooking sherry for her. We played Old Maid, Gin Rummy, Hearts. After that there was the sofa bed to be unfolded and the sour under-sheet pulled tight, and the blanket to be pinned up somehow from the ceiling to hang along the side of her bed for privacy. I lay and listened in helpless anger to her sighs, her snores, the squeaks of broken wind that she let off. Every other night, it seemed, I would wake to hear her as she wept, a knuckle pressed against her mouth and her face buried in the pillow. My father was rarely mentioned between us, unless he was late with the monthly postal order. She could not bring herself to speak his name; he was Gentleman Jim, or His Lordship, or, when she was in one of her rages or had taken too much sherry, Phil the Flute-player, or even Fart-arse the Fiddler. Her conceit was that he was enjoying a lavish success, *over there*, a success he cruelly refused to share with us as he should and as we deserved. The envelopes bringing the money orders – never a letter, only a card at Christmas or on my birthday, inscribed in the laboured copperplate of which he had always been so proud – bore the postmarks of places which even yet, when I am *over there* and see them signposted on the motorways his labour helped to build, provoke in me a confusion of feelings that includes a sticky sort of sadness, anger or its after-shock, and a curious yearning that is like nostalgia, a nostalgia for somewhere I have never been to. Watford. Coventry. Stoke. He too would have known the dingy rooms, the lino on the floor, the gas stove, the smells in the hall. Then the last letter came, from a strange woman – Maureen Strange, her name! – announcing *the very sad news I have to tell you*. My mother's bitter tears were as much of anger as of grief. 'Who's this,' she cried, 'this *Maureen*?' The single sheet of blue-lined notepaper shook in her hand. 'Blast him,' she said through gritted teeth, 'blast him anyway, the bastard!' In my mind I saw him for an instant, in the chalet, as it happens, at night, turning back from the open door in the thick yellow glow of the paraffin lamp and giving me an oddly quizzical glance, almost smiling, a spot of light from the lamp shining on his forehead and beyond him through the doorway the velvety depthless dark of the summer night.

Last thing, when the television stations are about to plunge into their unacceptably lurid late-night schedules, the set is firmly switched off and the Colonel has a cup of herbal tea prepared for him by Miss Vavasour. He tells me he hates the stuff – 'Not a word, mind!' – but dares not refuse. Miss Vavasour stands over him as he drinks. She insists it will help him sleep; he is gloomily convinced the opposite is the case, yet makes no protest, and drains the cup with a doomed expression. One night I persuaded him to accompany me to the Pier Head Bar for a nightcap, but it was a mistake. He grew anxious in my company – I did not blame him, I grow anxious in it myself – and fidgeted with his tobacco pipe and his glass of stout and kept easing back his cuff surreptitiously to check the time by his watch. The few locals who were there glowered at us, and we soon left, and walked back to the Cedars in silence under a tremendous October sky of stars and flying moon and tattered clouds. Most nights I drink myself to sleep, or attempt to, with half a dozen bumpers of brandy from the jeroboam of best Napoleon I keep in my room. I suppose I could offer him a drop of that, but I think not. The idea of late-night chats with the Colonel about life and related matters does not appeal. The night is long, my temper short.

Have I spoken already of my drinking? I drink like a fish. No, not like a fish, fishes do not drink, it is only breathing, their kind of breathing. I drink like one recently widowed – widowered? – a person of scant talent and scanter ambition, greyed o'er by the years, uncertain and astray and in need of consolation and the brief respite of drink-induced oblivion. I would take drugs if I had them, but I have not, and do not know how I might go about getting some. I doubt that Ballyless boasts a dope dealer. Perhaps the Pecker Devereux could help me. The Pecker is a fearsome fellow all shoulders and barrel chest with a big coarse weathered face and a gorilla's bandy arms. His huge face is pitted all over from some ancient acne or pox, each cavity ingrained with its speck of shiny black dirt. He used to be a deep-sea sailor, and is said to have killed a man. He has an orchard, where he lives in a wheelless caravan under the trees with his scrawny whippet of a wife. He sells apples and, clandestinely, a cloudy, sulphurous moonshine made from windfalls that sends the young men of the village crazy on Saturday nights. Why am I speaking of him like this? What is the Pecker Devereux to me? In these parts the x is pronounced, *Devrecks*, they say, I cannot stop. How wild the unguarded fancy runs.

Our day today was lightened, if that is the way to put it, by a visit from Miss Vavasour's friend Bun, who joined us for Sunday lunch. I came upon her at noon in the lounge, overflowing a wicker armchair in the bay window, lolling as if helpless there and faintly panting. The space where she sat was thronged with smoky sunlight and at first I could hardly make her out, although in truth she is as unmissable as the late Queen of Tonga. She is an enormous person, of indeterminate age. She wore a sack-coloured tweed dress tightly belted in the middle, which made her look as if she had been pumped up to bursting at bosom and hips, and her short stout cork-coloured legs were stuck out in front of her like two gigantic bungs protruding from her nether regions. A tiny sweet face, delicate of feature and pinkly aglow, is set in the big pale pudding of her head, the fossil remains, marvellously preserved, of the girl that she once was, long ago. Her ash-and-silver hair was done in an old-fashioned style, parted down the centre and pulled back into an eponymous bun. She smiled at me and nodded a greeting, her powdered wattles joggling. I did not know who she was, and thought she must be a guest newly arrived – Miss Vavasour has half a dozen vacant rooms for rent at this off-peak season. When she tottered to her feet the wicker chair cried out in excruciated relief. She really is of a prodigious bulk. I thought that if her belt buckle were to fail and the belt snap her trunk would flop into a perfectly spherical shape with her head on top like a large cherry on a, well, on a bun. It was apparent from the look she gave me, of mingled sympathy and eager interest, that she was aware of who I was and had been apprised of my stricken state. She told me her name, grand-sounding, with a hyphen, but I immediately forgot it. Her hand was small and soft and moistly warm, a baby's hand. Colonel Blunden came into the room then, with the

Sunday papers under his arm, and looked at her and frowned. When he frowns like that the yellowish whites of his eyes seem to darken and his mouth takes on the out-thrust blunt squareness of a muzzle.

Among the more or less harrowing consequences of bereavement is the sheepish sense I have of being an impostor. After Anna died I was everywhere attended upon, deferred to, made an object of special consideration. A hush surrounded me among people who had heard of my loss, so that I had no choice but to observe in return a solemn and pensive silence of my own, that very quickly set me twitching. It started, this singling-out, at the cemetery, if not before. With what tenderness they gazed at me across the grave-mouth, and how gently yet firmly they took my arm when the ceremony was done, as if I might be in danger of falling in a faint and pitching headlong into the hole myself. I even thought I detected a speculative something in the warmth with which certain of the women embraced me, in the lingering way they held on to my hand, gazing into my eyes and shaking their heads in wordless commiseration, with that melting stoniness of expression that old-style tragic actresses would put on in the closing scene when the harrowed hero staggered on stage with the heroine's corpse in his arms. I felt

I should stop and hold up a hand and tell these people that really, I did not deserve their reverence, for reverence is what it felt like, that I had been merely a bystander, a bit-player, while Anna did the dying. Throughout lunch Bun insisted on addressing me in tones of warm concern, muted awe, and try as I might I could modulate no tone in response that did not sound brave and bashful. Miss Vavasour, I could see, was finding all this gush increasingly annoying, and made repeated attempts to foster a less soulful, brisker atmosphere at the table, without success. The Colonel was no help, although he did try, breaking in on Bun's relentless flow of solicitude with weather forecasts and topics from the day's papers, but every time was rebuffed. He was simply no match for Bun. Showing his tarnished dentures in a ghastly display of grins and grimaces, he had the look of a hyena bobbing and squirming before the heedless advance of a hippo.

Bun lives in the city, in a flat over a shop, in circumstances which, she would firmly have me know, are far beneath her, daughter of the hyphenated gentry that she is. She reminds me of one of those hearty virgins of a bygone age, the housekeeping sister, say, of a bachelor clergyman or widowed squire. As she twittered on I pictured her in bombazine, whatever that is, and button-boots, seated in state on granite steps before a vast front door in the midst of a tiered array of squint-eyed domestics; I saw her, the fox's nemesis, in hunting pink and bowler hat with a veil, astride the sagging back of a big black galloping horse; or there she was in an enormous kitchen with range and scrubbed deal table and hanging hams, instructing loyal old Mrs Grub on which cuts of beef to serve for the Master's annual dinner to mark the Glorious Twelfth. Diverting myself in this harmless fashion I did not notice the fight developing between her and Miss Vavasour until it was well under way, and I had no idea how it might have started or what it was about. The two normally muted spots of colour on Miss Vavasour's cheekbones were burning fiercely, while Bun, who seemed to be swelling to even larger proportions under the pneumatic effects of a growing indignation, sat regarding her friend across the table with a fixed, froggy smile, her breath coming in fast little plosive gasps. They spoke with vengeful politeness, barging at each other like an unfairly matched pair of hobby-horses. *Really, I fail to see how you can say . . . Am I to understand that you . . .? The point is not that I . . . The point is that you did . . . Well, that is just . . . It most certainly is not . . . Excuse me, it most certainly is!*

The Colonel, increasingly alarmed, looked wildly from one of them to the other and back again, his eyes clicking in their sockets, as if he were watching a tennis match that had started in friendly enough fashion but had suddenly turned murderous.

I would have thought Miss Vavasour would emerge the easy victor from this contest, but she did not. She was not fighting with the full force of the weaponry I am sure she has at her command. Something, I could see, was holding her back, something of which Bun was well aware and which she leaned upon with all her considerable weight and to her strong advantage. Although they seemed in the heat of the argument to have forgotten about the Colonel and me, the realisation slowly dawned that they were conducting this struggle at least partly for my benefit, to impress me, and to try to win me over, to one side or the other. I could tell this from the manner in which Bun's little eager black eyes kept flickering coyly in my direction, while Miss Vavasour refused to glance my way even once. Bun, I began to see, was far more sly and astute than I would at first have given her credit for. One is inclined to imagine that people who are fat must also be stupid. This fat person, however, had taken the measure of me, and, I was convinced, saw me clearly for what I was, in all my essentials. And what was it that she saw? In my life it never troubled me to be kept by a rich, or richish, wife. I was born to be a dilettante, all that was lacking was the means, until I met Anna. Nor am I concerned particularly about the provenance of Anna's money, which was first Charlie Weiss's and is now mine, or how much or what kind of heavy machinery Charlie had to buy and sell in the making of it. What is money, after all? Almost nothing, when one has a sufficiency of it. So why was I squirming like this under Bun's veiled but knowing, irresistible scrutiny?

But come now, Max, come now. I will not deny it, I was always ashamed of my origins, and even still it requires only an arch glance or a condescending word from the likes of Bun to set me quivering inwardly in indignation and hot resentment. From the start I was bent on bettering myself. What was it that I wanted from Chloe Grace but to be on the level of her family's superior social position, however briefly, at whatever remove? It was hard going, scaling those Olympian heights. Sitting there with Bun I recalled with an irresistible faint shudder another Sunday lunch at the Cedars, half a century before. Who had invited me? Not Chloe, surely. Perhaps her mother did, when I was still her admirer and it amused her to have me sitting tongue-tied at her table. How nervous I was, really terrified. There were things on the table such as I had never seen before, odd-shaped cruets, china sauce-boats, a silver stand for the carving knife, a carving fork with a bone handle and a safety lever that could be pulled out at the back. As each course arrived I waited to see which pieces of cutlery the others would pick up before I would risk picking up my own. Someone passed me a bowl of mint sauce and I did not know what to do with it – mint sauce! Now and then from the other end of the table Carlo Grace, chewing vigorously, would bend a lively gaze on me. What was life like at the chalet, he wanted to know. What did we cook on? A Primus stove, I told him. 'Ha!' he cried. 'Primus *inter pares*!' And how he laughed, and Myles laughed too, and even Rose's lips twitched, though no one save he, I am sure, understood the sally, and Chloe scowled, not at their mockery but at my haplessness.

Anna could not sympathise with my sensitivities in these matters, she being the product of a classless class. She thought my mother a delight – fearsome, that is, unrelenting, and unforgiving, but for all that delightful, in her way. My mother, I need hardly say, did not reciprocate this warm regard. They met no more than two or three times, disastrously, I thought. Ma did not come to the wedding – let me admit it, I did not invite her – and died not long afterwards, at about the same time as Charlie Weiss. 'As if they were releasing us, the two of them,' Anna said. I did not share this benign interpretation, but made no comment. That was a day in the nursing home, she suddenly began to speak about my mother, with nothing to prompt her that I had noticed; the figures of the far past come back at the end, wanting their due. It was a morning after storm, and all outside the window of the corner room looked tousled and groggy, the dishevelled lawn littered with a caducous fall of leaves and the trees swaying still, like hungover drunks. On one wrist Anna wore a plastic tag and on the other a gadget like a wristwatch with a button that when pressed would release a fixed dose of morphine into her already polluted bloodstream. The first time we came home for a visit – home: the word gives me a shove, and I stumble – my mother hardly spoke a word to her. Ma was living in a flat by the canal, a dim low place that smelled of her landlady's cats. We had brought her gifts of duty-free cigarettes and a bottle of sherry, she accepted them with a sniff. She said she hoped we were not expecting her to put us up. We stayed in a cheap hotel nearby where the bath water was brown and Anna's handbag was stolen. We took Ma to the Zoo. She laughed at the baboons, nastily, letting us know they reminded her of someone, me, of course. One of them was masturbating, with a curiously lackadaisical air, looking off over its shoulder. 'Dirty thing,' Ma said dismissively and turned away.

We had tea in the café in the grounds, where the blaring of elephants mingled with the clamour of the bank holiday crowd. Ma smoked the duty-free cigarettes, ostentatiously stubbing each one out after three or four puffs, showing me what she thought of my peace offerings.

'Why does she keep calling you Max?' she hissed at me when Anna had gone to the counter to fetch a scone for her. 'Your name is not Max.'

'It is now,' I said. 'Did you not read the things I sent you, the things that I wrote, with my name printed on them?'

She gave one of her mountainous shrugs.

'I thought they were by somebody else.'

She could show her anger just by her way of sitting, skewed sideways on the chair, stiff-backed, her hands clamped on the handbag in her lap, her hat, shaped like a brioche and with a bit of black netting around the crown, askew on her unkempt grey curls. There was a little grey fuzz on her chin, too. She glanced contemptuously about her. 'Huh,' she said, 'this place. I suppose you'd like to leave me here, put me in with the monkeys and let them feed me bananas.'

Anna came back with the scone. Ma looked at it scornfully.

'I don't want that,' she said. 'I didn't ask for that.'

'Ma,' I said.

'Don't *Ma* me.'

But when we were leaving she wept, backing for cover behind the open door of the flat, lifting a forearm to hide her eyes, like a child, furious at herself. She died that winter, sitting on a bench by the canal one unseasonably mild mid-week afternoon. Angina pectoris, no one had known. The pigeons were still worrying at the crusts she had strewn for them on the path when a tramp sat down beside her and offered her a swig from his bottle in its brown-paper bag, not noticing she was dead.

'Strange,' Anna said. 'To be here, like that, and then not.'

She sighed, and looked out at the trees. They fascinated her, those trees, she wanted to go out and stand amongst them, to hear the wind blowing in the boughs. But there would be no going out, for her, any more. 'To have been here,' she said.

Someone was addressing me. It was Bun. How long had I been away, wandering through the chamber of horrors in my head? Lunch was done and Bun was saying goodbye. When she smiles her little face becomes smaller still, crinkling and contracting around the minute button of her nose. Through the window I could see clouds massing although a wettish sun low in the west still glared out of a pale sliver of leek-green sky. For a second I had that image of myself again, hunched hugely on my chair, pink lower lip adroop and enormous hands lying helplessly before me on the table, a great ape, captive, tranquillised and bleary. There are times, they occur with increasing frequency nowadays, when I seem to know nothing, when everything I did know seems to have fallen out of my mind like a shower of rain, and I am gripped for a moment in paralysed dismay, waiting for it all to come back but with no certainty that it will. Bun was gathering her things preparatory to the considerable effort of unbunging those mighty legs of hers from under the table and getting herself to her feet. Miss Vavasour had already risen and was hovering by her friend's shoulder – it was as big and round as a bowling-ball – impatient for her to be gone and trying not to show it. The Colonel was at Bun's other side, leaning forward at an awkward angle and making vague feints in the air with his hands, like a removals man squaring up to a weighty and particularly awkward item of furniture.

'Well!' Bun said, giving the table a tap with her knuckles, and looked up brightly first at Miss Vavasour, then at the Colonel, and both pressed a step more closely in, as if they might indeed be about to put a hand each under her elbows and heave her to her feet.

We went outside into the copper-coloured light of the late-autumn evening. Strong gusts of wind were sweeping up Station Road, making the tops of the trees thrash and flinging dead leaves about the sky. Rooks cawed rawly. The year is almost done. Why do I think something new will come to replace it, other than a number on a calendar? Bun's car, a nippy little red model, bright as a ladybird, was parked on the gravel inside the gate. It gasped on its springs as Bun inserted herself rearways into the driving seat, first pushing in her enormous behind then heaving up her legs and falling back heavily with a grunt against the fake tiger-skin upholstery. The Colonel drew open the gate for her and stood in the middle of the road and directed her out with broad dramatic sweeps of his arms. Smells of exhaust smoke, the sea, the garden's autumn rot. Brief desolation. I know nothing, nothing, old ape that I am. Bun sounded the car horn gaily and waved, her pinched face grinning through the glass at us, and Miss Vavasour waved back, not gaily, and the car buzzed away lopsidedly up the road and over the railway bridge and was gone.

'That's a perisher,' the Colonel said, rubbing his hands and heading indoors.

Miss Vavasour sighed.

We would have no dinner, lunch having lasted so long and having been so fraught. Miss V. was still agitated, I could see, from that bandying of words with her friend. When the Colonel followed her into the kitchen, angling for afternoon tea, at least, she was quite sharp with him, and he scuttled off to his room and the commentary to a football match on the wireless. I too retreated, to the lounge, with my book – Bell on Bonnard, dull as ditch-water – but I could not read, and put the book aside. Bun's visit had upset the delicate equilibrium of the household, there was a sort of noiseless trilling in the atmosphere, as if a fine, taut alarm wire had been tripped and was vibrating still. I sat in the bay of the window and watched the day darken. Bare trees across the road were black against the last flares of the setting sun, and the rooks in a raucous flock were wheeling and dropping, settling disputatiously for the night. I was thinking of Anna. I make myself think of her, I do it as an exercise. She is lodged in me like a knife and yet I am beginning to forget her. Already the image of her that I hold in my head is fraying, bits of pigments, flakes of gold leaf, are chipping off. Will the entire canvas be empty one day? I have come to realise how little I knew her, I mean how shallowly I knew her, how ineptly. I do not blame myself for this. Perhaps I should. Was I too lazy, too inattentive, too self-absorbed? Yes, all of those things, and yet I cannot think it is a matter of blame, this forgetting, this not-having-known. I fancy, rather, that I expected too much, in the way of knowing. I know so little of myself, how should I think to know another?

But wait, no, that is not it. I am being disingenuous – for a change, says you, yes yes. The truth is, we did not wish to know each other. More, what we wished was exactly that, not to know each other. I said somewhere already – no time to go back and look for it now, caught up all at once as I am in the toils of this thought – that what I found in Anna from the first was a way of fulfilling the fantasy of myself. I did not know quite what I meant when I said it, but thinking now on it a little I suddenly see. Or do I. Let me try to tease it out, I have plenty of time, these Sunday evenings are endless.

From earliest days I wanted to be someone else. The injunction *nosce te ipsum* had an ashen taste on my tongue from the first time a teacher enjoined me to repeat it after him. I knew myself, all too well, and did not like what I knew. Again, I must qualify. It was not what I was that I disliked, I mean the singular, essential me – although I grant that even the notion of an essential, singular self is problematic – but the congeries of affects, inclinations, received ideas, class tics, that my birth and upbringing had bestowed on me in place of a personality. In place of, yes. I never had a personality, not in the way that others have, or think they have. I was always a distinct no one, whose fiercest wish was to be an indistinct someone. I know what I mean. Anna, I saw at once, would be the medium of my transmutation. She was the fairground mirror in which all my distortions would be made straight. 'Why not be yourself?' she would say to me in our early days together – *be*, mark you, not *know* – pitying my fumbling attempts to grasp the great world. *Be yourself!* Meaning, of course, *Be anyone you like.* That was the pact we made, that we would relieve each other of the burden of being the people whom everyone else told us we were. Or at least she relieved me of that burden, but what did I do for her? Perhaps I should not include her in this drive towards unknowing, perhaps it was only I who desired ignorance.

The question I am left with now, anyway, is precisely the question of knowing. Who, if not ourselves, were we? All right, leave Anna out of it. Who, if not myself, was I? The philosophers tell us that we are defined and have our being through others. Is a rose red in the dark? In a forest on a far planet where there are no ears to hear does a falling tree make a crash? I ask: who was to know me, if not Anna? Who was to know Anna, if not I? Absurd questions. We were happy together, or not unhappy, which is more than most people manage; is that not enough? There were strains, there were stresses, as how would there not be in any union such as ours, if any such there are. The shouts, the screams, the flung plates, the odd slap, the odder punch, we had all that. Then there was Serge and his ilk, not to mention my Sergesses, no, not to mention. But even in our most savage fights we were only violently at play, like Chloe and Myles in their wrestling matches.

Our quarrels we ended in laughter, bitter laughter, but laughter all the same, abashed and even a little ashamed, ashamed that is not of our ferocity, but our lack of it. We fought in order to feel, and to feel real, being the self-made creatures that we were. That I was.

Could we, could I, have done otherwise? Could I have lived differently? Fruitless interrogation. Of course I could, but I did not, and therein lies the absurdity of even asking. Anyway, where are the paragons of authenticity against whom my concocted self might be measured? In those final bathroom paintings that Bonnard did of the septuagenarian Marthe he was still depicting her as the teenager he had thought she was when he first met her. Why should I demand more veracity of vision of myself than of a great and tragic artist? We did our best, Anna and I. We forgave each other for all that we were not. What more could be expected, in this vale of torments and tears? *Do not look so worried*, Anna said, *I hated you, too, a little, we were human beings, after all.* Yet for all that, I cannot rid myself of the conviction that we missed something, that I missed something, only I do not know what it might have been.

Lost track. Everything is mixed up. Why do I

torment myself with these insoluble equivocations, have I not had enough of casuistry? Leave yourself alone, Max, leave yourself alone.

Miss Vavasour came in, a moving wraith in the shadows of the twilit room. She enquired if I was warm enough, if she should light a fire. I asked her about Bun, who was she, how had they met, just for the sake of asking something. It was a while before she gave an answer, and when she did it was to a question I had not asked.

'Well, you see,' she said, 'Vivienne's people own this house.'

'Vivienne?'

'Bun.'

'Ah.'

She bent to the fireplace and lifted the bunch of dried hydrangea, crackling, from the grate.

'Or perhaps it is she who owns it now,' she said, 'since most of her people have passed on.' I said I was surprised, I had thought the house was hers. 'No,' she said, frowning at the brittle flowers in her hands, then looked up, almost impish, showing the tiniest tip of a tongue. 'But I come with it, so to speak.'

Faintly from the Colonel's room we heard the crowd cheering and the commentator's excited squawks; someone had scored a goal. They must be playing in the almost dark by now. Injury time.

'And you never married?' I said.

She smiled a frugal smile at that, casting down her eyes again.

'Oh, no,' she said. 'I never married.' She glanced at me quickly and away. The two spots of colour on her cheekbones glowed. 'Vivienne,' she said, 'was my friend. Bun, that is.'

'Ah,' I said again. What else could I say?

She is playing the piano now. Schumann, *Kinderszenen*. As if to prompt me.

Strange, is it not, the way they lodge in the mind, the seemingly inconsidered things? Behind the Cedars, where a corner of the house met the tussocked lawn, under a crooked black drainpipe, there stood a water butt, long gone by now, of course. It was a wooden barrel, a real one, full-size, the staves blackened with age and the iron hoops eaten to frills by rust. The rim was nicely bevelled, and so smooth that one could hardly feel the joins between the staves; smoothly sawn, that is, and planed, but in texture the sodden grain-end of the wood there was slightly furry, or napped, rather, like the pod of a bulrush, only tougher to the touch, and chillier, and more moist. Although it must have held I do not know how many scores of gallons it was always full almost to the brim, thanks to the frequency of rain in these parts, even, or especially, in summer. When I looked down into it the water seemed black and thick as oil. Because the barrel listed a little the surface of the water formed a fat ellipse, that trembled at the slightest breath and broke into terror-stricken ripples when a train went past. That ill-tended corner of the garden had a soft damp climate all of its own, due to the presence of the water barrel. Weeds in profusion flourished there, nettles, dock leaves, convolvulus, other things I do not know the name of, and the daylight had a greenish cast to it, particularly so in the morningtime. The water in the barrel, being rain water, was soft, or hard, one or the other, and therefore was considered good for the hair, or the scalp, or something, I do not know. And it was there one glittering sunny morning that I came upon Mrs Grace helping Rose to wash her hair.

Memory dislikes motion, preferring to hold things still, and as with so many of these remembered scenes I see this one as a tableau. Rose stands bent forward from the waist with her hands on her knees, her hair hanging down from her face in a long black shining wedge dripping with soap suds. She is barefoot, I see her toes in the long grass, and is wearing one of those vaguely Tyrolean short-sleeved white linen blouses that were so popular at the time, full at the waist and tight at the shoulders and embroidered across the bust in an abstract pattern of red and Prussian-blue stitching. The neckline is deeply scalloped and inside it I have a clear glimpse of her pendent breasts, small and spiked, like the business ends of two spinning-tops. Mrs Grace wears a blue satin dressing gown and delicate blue slippers, bringing an incongruous breath of the boudoir into the out-of-doors. Her hair is pinned back at the ears with two tortoise-shell clasps, or slides, I think they were called. It is apparent she is not long out of bed, and in the morning light her face has a raw, roughly sculpted look. She stands in the very pose of Vermeer's maid with the milk jug, her head and her left shoulder inclined, one hand cupped under the heavy fall of Rose's hair and the other pouring a dense silvery sluice of water from a chipped enamel jug. The water where it falls on the crown of Rose's head makes a bare patch that shakes and slithers, like the spot of moonlight on Pierrot's sleeve. Rose gives little hooting cries of protest – '*Oo! Oo! Oo!*' – at the cold shock of the water on her scalp.

Poor Rosie. I can never think of her name without that epithet attached. She was, what, nineteen, twenty at the most. Tallish, remarkably slender, narrow at waist and long of hip, she was possessed of a silky, sulky gracefulness from the height of her pale flat brow to her neat and shapely and slightly splay-toed feet. I suppose someone wishing to be unkind – Chloe, for instance – might have described her features as sharp. Her nose, with its tear-shaped, pharaonic nostrils, was prominent at the bridge, the skin stretched tight and translucent over the bone. It is deflected, this nose, a fraction to the left, so that when one looks at her straight-on there is the illusion of seeing her at once full-face and in profile, as in one of those fiddly Picasso portraits. This defect, far from making her seem misproportioned, only added to the soulful expressiveness of her face. In repose, when she was unaware of being spied on – and what a little spy I was! – she would hold her head at an acute downward tilt, her eyes hooded and her shallowly cleft chin tucked into her shoulder. Then she would seem a Duccio madonna, melancholy, remote, self-forgetting, lost in the sombre dream of all that was to come, of all that, for her, was not to come.

Of the three central figures in that summer's salt-bleached triptych it is she, oddly, who is most sharply delineated on the wall of my memory. I think the reason for this is that the first two figures in the scene, I mean Chloe and her mother, are all my own work while Rose is by another, unknown, hand. I keep going up close to them, the two Graces, now mother, now daughter, applying a dab of colour here, scumbling a detail there, and the result of all this close work is that my focus on them is blurred rather than sharpened, even when I stand back to survey my handiwork. But Rose, Rose is a completed portrait, Rose is done. This does not mean she was more real or of more significance to me than Chloe or her mother, certainly not, only that I can picture her with the most immediacy. It cannot be because she is still here, for the version of her which is here is so changed as to be hardly recognisable. I see her in her pumps and sheer black pants and shirt of a crimson shade – although she must have had other outfits, this is the one she wears in almost every one of my recollections of her – posed among inconsequentials, the arbitrary props of the studio, a dull drape, a dusty straw hat with a blossom in the band, a bit of mossed-over wall that is probably made of cardboard, and, high up in one corner, an umber doorway where, mysteriously, deep shadows give on to a white-gold blaze of empty light. Her presence was not as vivid for me as that of Chloe or Mrs Grace, how could it be, yet there was something that set her apart, with that midnight-black hair of hers and that white skin the powdery bloom of which the strongest sunlight or harshest sea breeze seemed incapable of smudging.

She was I suppose what in the old days, I mean days even older than those of which I speak, would have been called a governess. A governess, however, would have had her modest spheres of power, but poor Rosie was helpless before the twins and their unheeding parents. For Chloe and Myles she was the obvious enemy, the butt of their cruellest jokes, an object of resentment and endless ridicule. They had two modes by which they treated her. They were either indifferent, to the point that she might have been invisible to them, or else they subjected everything she did or said, however trivial, to a relentless scrutiny and interrogation. As she moved about the house they would follow after her, crowding on her heels, watching closely her every action – putting down a plate, picking up a book, trying not to look at herself in a mirror – as if what she was doing were the most outlandish and inexplicable behaviour they had ever witnessed. She would ignore them for as long as she could bear but in the end would turn on them, flushed and trembling, and implore them please, please, to leave her alone, keeping her voice to an anguished whisper for fear the elder Graces should hear her losing control. This was just the response the twins had wanted, of course, and they would press up to her more closely still and peer eagerly into her face, feigning wonderment, and Chloe would bombard her with questions – what had been on the plate? was that a good book? why did she not want to see herself in the glass? – until tears welled up in her eyes and her mouth sagged askew in sorrow and impotent rage, and then the two of them would run off in delight, laughing like demons.

I discovered Rose's secret one Saturday afternoon when I came to the Cedars to call for Chloe. As I arrived she was getting into the car with her father and about to leave for a trip to town. I stopped at the gate. We had made an arrangement to go and play tennis – could she have forgotten? Of course she could. I was dismayed; to be abandoned like this on an empty Saturday afternoon was not a thing lightly to be borne. Myles, who was opening the gate for his father to drive through, saw my dismay and grinned, like the malignant sprite that he was. Mr Grace peered out at me from behind the windscreen and inclined his head towards Chloe and said something, and he also was grinning. By now the day itself, breezy and bright, seemed to exude derision and a generalised merriment. Mr Grace trod hard on the accelerator and the car with a loud report from its hindquarters bounded forward on the gravel so that I had to step smartly out of the way – although they shared nothing else, my father and Carlo Grace had the same truculently playful sense of fun – and Chloe through the side window, her face blurred behind the glass, looked out at me with an expression of frowning surprise, as if she had just that moment noticed me standing there, which for all I knew she had. I waved a hand, with as much carelessness as I could feign, and she smiled with down-turned mouth in a fakely rueful way and gave an exaggerated shrug of apology, lifting her shoulders level with her ears. The car had slowed for Myles to get in and she put her face close to the window and mouthed something, and raised her left hand in an oddly formal gesture, it might have been a sort of blessing, and what could I do but smile and shrug too, and wave again, as she was borne away in a swirl of exhaust smoke, with Myles's severed-seeming head in the rear window, grinning back at me gloatingly.

The house had a deserted aspect. I walked past the front door and down to where the diagonal row of trees marked the end of the garden. Beyond was the railway line paved with jagged loose blue shale and giving off its mephitic whiff of ash and gas. The trees, planted too close together, were spindly and misshapen, their highest branches confusedly waving like so many arms upflung in wild disorder. What were they? Not oaks – sycamores, perhaps. Before I knew what I was doing I was clambering up the middlemost one. This was not like me, I was not daring or adventurous, and had, and have, no head for heights. Up I went, however, up and up, hand and instep, instep and hand, from bough to bough. The climb was exhilaratingly easy, despite the foliage hissing in scandalised protest around me and twigs slapping at my face, and soon I was as near the top as it was possible to go. There I clung, fearless as any jack tar astride the rigging, the earth's deck gently rolling far below me, while, above, a low sky of dull pearl seemed close enough to touch. At this height the breeze was a steady flow of solid air, smelling of inland things, earth, and smoke, and animals. I could see the roofs of the town on the horizon, and farther off and higher up, like a mirage, a tiny silver ship propped motionless on a smear of pale sea. A bird landed on a twig and looked at me in surprise and then flew away again quickly with an offended chirp.

I had by now forgotten Chloe's forgetfulness, so exultant was I and brimful of manic glee at being so high and so far from everything, and I did not notice Rose below me until I heard her sobbing.

She was standing underneath the tree next to the one in which I was perched, her shoulders hunched and her elbows pressed into her sides as if to keep herself upright. Her agitated fingers clutched a wadded handkerchief, but so novelettishly was she posed, weeping there amidst the soughing airs of afternoon, that I thought at first it must be a crumpled love letter and not a hankie she was holding. How odd she looked, foreshortened to an irregular disc of shoulders and head – the parting in her hair was the same shade of off-white as the sodden handkerchief she was holding – and when she turned hastily at the sound of a step behind her she wobbled briefly like a ninepin that the bowl has succeeded only in striking a glancing blow. Mrs Grace was approaching along the pathway worn in the grass under the clothesline, her head bowed and her arms folded cruciform over flattened breasts and a hand clasped crosswise on each shoulder. She was barefoot, and wore shorts, and one of her husband's white shirts that was flatteringly far too big for her. She stopped a little way off from Rose and stood a moment silent, turning from side to side in quarter-turns on the pivot of herself, still with her hands on her shoulders, as if she too like Rose were holding herself up, herself a child that she was rocking in her arms.

'Rose,' she said in a playfully coaxing tone, 'oh, Rose, what is it?'

Rose, who had resolutely turned her face to the far fields again, gave a liquid snort of not-laughter.

'What is it?' she cried, her voice flying up on the final word and spilling over on itself. 'What is it?'

She blew her nose indignantly on the rim of the balled-up hankie and finished with a hair-tossing snuffle. Even from this angle I could see that Mrs Grace was smiling, and biting her lip. Behind me from afar came a hooting whistle. The afternoon train from town, matt-black engine and half a dozen green wooden carriages, was blundering towards us through the fields like a big mad toy, huffing bulbous links of thick white smoke. Mrs Grace moved forward soundlessly and touched a fingertip to Rose's elbow but Rose snatched her arm away as if the touch were burning hot. A flurry of wind flattened the shirt against Mrs Grace's body and showed distinctly the fat outlines of her breasts. 'Oh, come on now, Rosie,' she coaxed again, and this time managed to insinuate a hand into the crook of the girl's arm and with a series of soft tugs made her turn, stiff and unwilling though she was, and together they set off pacing under the trees. Rose went stumblingly, talking and talking, while Mrs Grace kept her head down as before and seemed hardly to speak at all; from the set of her shoulders and a stooping drag to her gait I suspected she was suppressing an urge to laugh. Of Rose's tremulous hiccupy words the ones I caught were *love* and *foolish* and *Mr Grace*, and of Mrs Grace's responses only a shouted *Carlo?* followed by an incredulous whoop. Suddenly the train was there, making the trunk of the tree vibrate between my knees; as the engine passed I looked into the cabin and saw distinctly the white of an eye flash up at me from under a gleaming, smoke-blackened brow. When I turned back to them the two had stopped pacing and stood face to face in the long grass, Mrs Grace smiling with a hand lifted to Rose's shoulder and Rose, her nostrils edged with pink, gouging into her teary eyes with the knuckles of both hands, and then a blinding plume of the train's smoke blew violently into my face and by the time it cleared they had turned and were walking back up the path together to the house.

So there it was. Rose was lost in love for the father of the children in her charge. It was the old story, although I do not know how it was old for me, who was so young. What did I think, what feel? I recall most clearly the wadded handkerchief in Rose's hands and the blue filigree of incipient varicose veins on the backs of Mrs Grace's strong bare calves. And the steam engine, of course, that had come to a clanking stop over in the station, and stood now seething and gasping and squirting jets of scalding water from its fascinatingly intricate underparts as it waited impatiently to be off again. What are living beings, compared to the enduring intensity of mere things?

When Rose and Mrs Grace were gone I climbed down from the tree, a harder thing to do than climbing up had been, and went softly past the silent and unseeing house and walked down Station Road in the polished pewter light of the emptied afternoon. That train had pulled out of the station and by now was already somewhere else, somewhere else entirely.

Naturally I lost no time in telling Chloe of my discovery. Her response was not at all what I had expected it would be. True, she seemed shocked at first, but quickly assumed a sceptical air, and even appeared to be annoyed, I mean annoyed at me, for having told her. This was disconcerting. I had depended on her greeting my account of the scene under the trees with a delighted cackle, which in turn would have allowed me the assurance to treat the matter as a joke, instead of which I was forced to reflect on it in a more serious and sombre light. A sombre light, imagine that. But why a joke? Because laughter, for the young, is a neutralising force, and tames terrors? Rose, although nearly twice as old as we were, was still on this side of the gulf that separated us from the world of the adults. It was bad enough to have to entertain the thought of them, the real grown-ups, at their furtive frolics, but the possibility of Rose cavorting with a man of Carlo Grace's years – that paunch, that bulging crotch, that chest-fur with its glints of grey – was hardly to be entertained by a sensibility as delicate, as callow, as mine still was. Had she declared her love to Mr Grace? Had he reciprocated? The pictures that flashed before me of pale Rose reclining in her satyr's rough embrace excited and alarmed me in equal measure. And what of Mrs Grace? How calmly she had received Rose's blurted confession, with what lightness, what amusement, even. Why had she not scratched out the girl's eyes with her glistening, vermilion claws?

Then there were the lovers themselves. How I marvelled at the ease, the smooth effrontery, with which they masked all that was going on between them. Carlo Grace's very insouciance seemed now a mark of criminal intent. Who but a heartless seducer would laugh like that, and tease, and thrust out his chin and scratch rapidly in the grizzled beard underneath it, his fingernails making a rasping sound? The fact that in public he paid no more attention to Rose than he did to anyone else who happened to cross his path was only a further sign of his cunning and his skilful dissimulation. Rose had only to hand him his newspaper, and he had only to accept it from her, for it to seem to my hotly vigilant eye that a clandestine, indecent exchange had taken place. Her mild and diffident demeanour in his presence was to me that of a debauched nun, now that I knew of her secret shame, and images moved in the deeper reaches of my imagination of her glimmering pale form joined with him in dim coarse couplings, and I heard his muffled bellows and her muted moans of dark delight.

What had driven her to confess, and to her beloved's spouse, at that? And what did she think, poor Rosie, the first time her eye fell on the slogan that Myles scrawled in chalk on the gate posts and on

234

the footpath outside the gate – *RV loves CG* – and the accompanying rudimentary sketch of a female torso, two circles with dots in the centre, two curves for the flanks, and, below, a pair of brackets enclosing a curt, vertical gash? She must have blushed, oh, she must have burned. She thought it was Chloe, not I, who had somehow found her out. Strangely, though, it was not Chloe whose power was thus increased over Rose, but the contrary, or so it seemed. The governess's eye had a new and steelier light when it fell on the girl now, and the girl, to my surprise and puzzlement, appeared cowed under that look as she had never been before. When I think of them like that, the one glinting, the other shying, I cannot but speculate that what happened on the day of the strange tide was in some way a consequence of the uncovering of Rose's secret passion. After all, why should I be less susceptible than the next melodramatist to the tale's demand for a neat closing twist?

The tide came up the beach all the way to the foot of the dunes, as though the sea were brimming over its bounds. In silence we watched the water's steady advance, sitting in a row, the three of us, Chloe and Myles and me, with our backs against the peeling grey boards of the disused groundsman's hut beside the first tee of the golf course. We had been swimming but we had given up, made uneasy by this waveless, unstoppable tide, the sinister, calm way it kept coming on. The sky was misted white all over with a flat, pale-gold disc of sun stuck motionless in the middle of it. Gulls swooped, shrieking. The air was still. Yet I distinctly recall how the single blades of marram grass growing up through the sand round-about had each inscribed a neat half circle in front of itself, which suggests a wind was blowing, or at least a breeze. Perhaps that was another day, the day I noticed the grass marking the sand like that. Chloe was in her swimsuit, with a white cardigan draped over her shoulders. Her hair was darkly wet and plastered to her skull. In that unshadowed milky light her face seemed almost featureless, and she and Myles beside her were as alike as the profiles on a pair of coins. Below us in a hollow in the dunes Rose lay on her back on a beach towel with her hands behind her head and seemed to be asleep. The sea's scummed edge was within a yard of her heels. Chloe considered her, smiling to herself. 'Maybe she'll be washed away,' she said.

It was Myles who got the door of the hut open, twisting the padlock until the bolt broke from its screws and came away in his hand. Inside, there was a single tiny room, empty, and smelling of old urine.

A wooden bench seat was set along one wall, and above it there was a small window, the frame intact but the glass long gone. Chloe knelt on the bench with her face in the window and her elbows on the sill. I sat on one side of her, Myles on the other. Why do I think there was something Egyptian about the way that we were posed there, Chloe kneeling and looking out and Myles and I on the bench and facing into the little room? Is it because I am compiling a Book of the Dead? She was the Sphinx and we her seated priests. There was silence, save for the crying of the gulls.

'I hope she gets drowned,' Chloe said, speaking through the window, and gave one of her sharp little nicking laughs. 'I hope she does' – *nick nick* – 'I hate her.'

Last words. It was early morning, just before dawn, when Anna came to consciousness. I could not rightly tell if I had been awake or just dreaming that I was. Those nights that I spent sprawled in the armchair beside her bed were rife with curiously mundane hallucinations, half dreams of preparing meals for her, or talking about her to people I had never seen before, or just walking along with her, through dim, nondescript streets, I walking, that is, and she lying comatose beside me and yet managing to move, and keep pace with me, somehow, sliding along on solid air, on her journey towards the Field of Reeds. Waking now, she turned her head on the damp pillow and looked at me wide-eyed in the underwater glimmer of the nightlight with an expression of large and wary startlement. I think she did not know me. I had that paralysing sensation, part awe and part alarm, that comes over one in a sudden and unexpected solitary encounter with a creature of the wild. I could feel my heart beating in slow, liquid thumps, as if it were flopping over an endless series of identical obstacles. Anna coughed, making a sound like the clatter of bones. I knew this was the end. I felt inadequate to the moment, and wanted to cry out for help. Nurse, nurse, come quick, my wife is leaving me! I could not think, my mind seemed filled with toppling masonry. Still Anna stared at me, still surprised, still suspicious. Away down the corridor someone unseen dropped something that clattered, she heard the noise and seemed reassured. Perhaps she thought it was something I had said, and thought she understood it, for she nodded, but impatiently, as if to say *No, you're wrong, that is not it at all!* She reached out a hand and fixed it claw-like on my wrist. That monkeyish grasp, it holds me yet. I blundered forward from the chair in a sort of panic and scrambled to my knees beside the bed, like one of the dumbstruck faithful falling in adoration before an apparition. Anna was still clutching my wrist. I put my other hand on her brow, and it seemed to me I could feel her mind behind it feverishly at work, making the last tremendous effort of thinking its final thought. Had I ever looked at her in life, with such urgent attention, as I looked at her now? As if looking alone would hold her here, as if she could not go so long as my eye did not flinch. She was panting, softly and slowly, like a runner pausing who still has miles to run. Her breath gave off a mild, dry stink, as of withered flowers. I spoke her name but she only closed her eyes briefly, dismissively, as if I should know that she was no longer Anna, that she was no longer anyone, and then opened them and stared at me again, harder than ever, not in surprise now but with a commanding sternness, willing that I should hear, hear and understand, what it was she had to say. She let go of my wrist and her fingers scrabbled briefly on the bed, searching for something. I took her hand. I could feel the flutter of a pulse at the base of her thumb. I said something, some fatuous thing such as *Don't go*, or *Stay with me*, but again she gave that impatient shake of the head, and tugged my hand to draw me closer. 'They are stopping the clocks,' she said, the merest thread of a whisper, conspiratorial. 'I have stopped time.' And she nodded, a solemn, knowing nod, and smiled, too, I would swear it was a smile.

It was the deft, brusque way that Chloe shrugged off her cardigan that prompted me, that permitted me, to put my hand against the back of her thigh where she knelt beside me. Her skin was chill and stippled with gooseflesh but I could feel the busy blood swarming just below the surface. She did not respond to my touch but went on looking out at whatever it was she was looking at – all that water, perhaps, that inexorable slow flood – and cautiously I slid my hand upward until my fingers touched the taut hem of her bathing suit. Her cardigan, that had settled on my lap, now slithered off and tumbled to the floor, making me think of something, a spray of flowers let fall, perhaps, or a falling bird. It would have been enough for me just to go on sitting there with my hand under her bottom, my heart beating out a syncopated measure and my eyes fixed on a knot-hole in the wooden wall opposite, had she not in a tiny, convulsive movement shifted her knee a fraction sideways along the bench and opened her lap to my astonished fingertips. The wadded crotch of her swimsuit was sopping with sea water that felt scalding to my touch. No sooner had my fingers found her there than she clenched her thighs shut again, trapping my hand. Shivers like tiny electric currents ran from all over her into her lap, and with a wriggle she pulled herself free of me, and I thought it was all over, but I was wrong. Quickly she turned about and climbed down from the bench all knees and elbows and sat beside me squirmingly and turned up her face and offered me her cold lips and hot mouth to kiss. The straps of her swimsuit were tied in a bow at the back of her neck, and now without moving her mouth from mine she put up a hand behind her and undid the knot and tugged the wet cloth down to her waist. Still kissing her, I inclined my head to the side and looked with the eye that could see past her ear down along the ridges of her spine to the beginnings of her narrow rump and the cleft there the colour of a clean steel knife. With an impatient gesture she took my hand and pressed it to the barely perceptible mound of one of her breasts the tip of which was cold and hard. On her other side Myles sat with his legs loosely splayed before him, leaning his head back against the wall with his eyes closed. Blindly Chloe reached out sideways and found his hand lying palm-upwards on the bench and clasped it, and as she did so her mouth tightened against mine and I felt rather than heard the faint mewling moan that rose in her throat.

I did not hear the door opening, only registered the light altering in the little room. Chloe stiffened against me and turned her head quickly and said something, a word I did not catch. Rose was standing in the doorway. She was in her bathing suit but was wearing her black pumps, which made her long pale skinny legs seem even longer and paler and skinnier. She reminded me of something, I could not think what, one hand on the door and the other on the door-jamb, seeming to be held suspended there between two strong gusts, one from inside the hut driving against her and another from outside pressing at her back. Chloe hastily pulled up the flap of her swimsuit and retied the straps behind her neck, speaking that word again harshly under her breath, the word I could not catch – Rose's name, was it, or just some imprecation? – and made a low dive from the bench, fast as a fox, and ducked under Rose's arm and was gone through the door and away. 'You come back here, Miss!' Rose cried in a voice that cracked. 'Just you come back here this instant!' She gave me a look then, a more-in-sorrow-than-in-anger look, and shook her head, and turned and stalked off stork-like on those stilted white legs. Myles, still sprawled on the bench beside me, gave a low laugh. I stared at him. It seemed to me that he had spoken.

All that followed I see in miniature, in a sort of cameo, or one of those rounded views, looked on from above, at the off-centre of which the old painters would depict the moment of a drama in such tiny detail as hardly to be noticed amidst the blue and gold expanses of sea and sky. I lingered a moment on the bench, breathing. Myles watched me, waiting to see what I would do. When I came out of the hut Chloe and Rose were down on the little semi-circle of sand between the dunes and the water's edge, squared up to each other and shrieking in each other's face. I could not hear what they were saying. Now Chloe broke away and stamped in a furious, tight ring around herself, churning the sand. She kicked Rose's towel. It is only my fancy, I know, but I see the little waves lapping hungrily at her heels. At last, with one last cry and a curious, chopping gesture of a hand and forearm, she turned and walked to the edge of the waves and, scissoring her legs, plumped down on the sand and sat with her knees pressed against her breast and her arms wrapped about her knees, her face lifted towards the horizon. Rose with hands on hips stood glaring at her back, but seeing she would get no response turned away and began angrily to gather up her things, pitching towel, book, bathing cap into the crook of her arm like a fishwife throwing fish into a creel. I heard Myles behind me, and a second later he passed me by at a headlong sprint, seeming to cartwheel rather than run. When he got to where Chloe was sitting he sat down beside her and put an arm across her shoulders and laid his head against hers. Rose paused and cast an uncertain glance at them, wrapped there together, their backs turned to the world. Then calmly they stood up and waded into the sea, the water smooth as oil hardly breaking around them, and leaned forward in unison and swam out slowly, their two heads bobbing on the whitish swell, out, and out.

We watched them, Rose and I, she clutching her gathered-up things against her, and I just standing. I do not know what I was thinking, I do not remember thinking anything. There are times like that, not frequent enough, when the mind just empties. They were far out now, the two of them, so far as to be pale dots between pale sky and paler sea, and then one of the dots disappeared. After that it was all over very quickly, I mean what we could see of it. A splash, a little white water, whiter than that all around, then nothing, the indifferent world closing.

There was a shout, and Rose and I turned to see

a large red-faced man with close-clipped grey hair coming down the dunes towards us, high-stepping flurriedly through the sliding sands with comical haste. He wore a yellow shirt and khaki trousers and two-tone shoes and was brandishing a golf club. The shoes I may have invented. I am sure however of the glove that he wore on his right hand, the hand that held the golf stick; it was light brown, fingerless, and the back of it was punched with holes, I do not know why it caught my attention particularly. He kept shouting that someone should go for the Guards. He seemed extremely angry, gesturing in the air with the club like a Zulu warrior shaking his knobkerrie. Zulus, knobkerries? Perhaps I mean assegais. His caddy, meanwhile, up on the bank, an ageless emaciated runt in a buttoned-up tweed jacket and a tweed cap, stood contemplating the scene below him with a sardonic expression, leaning casually on the golf bag with his ankles crossed. Next, a muscle-bound young man in tight blue swimming trunks appeared, I do not know from where, he seemed to materialise out of the very air, and without preliminary plunged into the sea and swam out swiftly with expert, stiff strokes. By now Rose was pacing back and forth at the water's edge, three paces this way, stop, wheel, three paces that way, stop, wheel, like poor demented Ariadne on the Naxos shore, still clutching to her breast the towel, book and bathing cap. After a time the would-be life-saver came back, and strode towards us out of the waveless water with that swimmer's hindered swagger, shaking his head and snorting. It was no go, he said, no go. Rose cried out, a sort of sob, and shook her head rapidly from side to side, and the golfer glared at her. Then they were all dwindling behind me, for I was running, trying to run, along the beach, in the direction of Station Road and the Cedars. Why did I not cut away, through the grounds of the Golf Hotel, on to the road, where the going would have been so much easier? But I did not want the going to be easier. I did not want to get where I was going. Often in my dreams I am back there again, wading through that sand that grows ever more resistant, so that it seems that my feet them-selves are made of some massy, crumbling stuff. What did I feel? Most strongly, I think, a sense of awe, awe of myself, that is, who had known two living crea-tures that now were suddenly, astoundingly, dead. But did I believe they were dead? In my mind they were held suspended in a vast bright space, upright, their arms linked and their eyes wide open, gazing gravely before them into illimitable depths of light.

Here at last was the green iron gate, the car

standing on the gravel, and the front door, wide open as so often. In the house all was tranquil and still. I moved among the rooms as if I were myself a thing of air, a drifting spirit, Ariel set free and at a loss. I found Mrs Grace in the living room. She turned to me, putting a hand to her mouth, the milky light of afternoon at her back. This all is silence, save for the drowsy hum of summer from without. Then Carlo Grace came in, saying, 'Damned thing, it seems to be . . .' and he stopped too, and so we stood in stillness, we three, at the end.

Was't well done?

Night, and everything so quiet, as if there were no one, not even myself. I cannot hear the sea, which on other nights rumbles and growls, now near and grating, now afar and faint. I do not want to be alone like this. Why have you not come back to haunt me? It is the least I would have expected of you. Why this silence day after day, night after interminable night? It is like a fog, this silence of yours. First it was a blur on the horizon, the next minute we were in the midst of it, purblind and stumbling, clinging to each other. It started that day after the visit to Mr Todd when we walked out of the clinic into the deserted car park, all those machines ranked neatly there, sleek as porpoises and making not a sound, and no sign even of the young woman and her clicking high heels. Then our house shocked into its own kind of silence, and soon thereafter the silent corridors of hospitals, the hushed wards, the waiting rooms, and then the last room of all. Send back your ghost. Torment me, if you like. Rattle your chains, drag your cerements across the floor, keen like a banshee, anything. I would have a ghost.

Where is my bottle. I need my big baby's bottle. My soother.

Miss Vavasour gives me a pitying look. I blench under her glance. She knows the questions I want to ask, the questions I have been burning to put to her since I first came here but never had the nerve. This morning when she saw me silently formulating them yet again she shook her head, not unkindly. 'I can't help you,' she said, smiling. 'You must know that.' What does she mean by must? I know so little of anything. We are in the lounge, sitting in the bay of the bow window, as so often. The day outside is bright and cold, the first real day of winter we have had. All this in the historic present. Miss Vavasour is mending what looks suspiciously like one of the Colonel's socks. She has a wooden gadget, shaped like a large mushroom, on which she stretches the heel to darn the hole in it. I find it restful to watch her at this timeless task. I am in need of rest. My head might be packed with wet cotton wool and there is an acid taste of vomit in my mouth which all Miss Vavasour's plyings of milky tea and soldiers of thin-sliced toast cannot rid me of. Also there is a bruise on my temple that throbs. I sit before Miss V. sheepish and contrite. I feel more than ever the delinquent boy.

But what a day it was yesterday, what a night, and, heavens! what a morning-after. It all began with fair enough promise. Ironically, as it would turn out, it was the Colonel's daughter who was supposed to come down, along with Hubby and the children. The Colonel tried to be nonchalant, putting on his gruffest manner – 'We'll be rightly invaded!' – but over breakfast his hands shook so with excitement that he set the table to trembling and the tea cups rattling in their saucers. Miss Vavasour insisted that his daughter and her family should all stay for lunch, that she would cook a chicken, and asked what kind of ice cream the children would like. 'Oh, now,' the Colonel blustered, 'really, there's no need!' It was plain to see he was deeply affected, however, and was damp-eyed for a moment. I looked forward myself with some anticipation to getting a look at last at this daughter and her he-man husband. The prospect of the children was somewhat daunting, though; kiddies in general, I am afraid, bring out the not so latent Gilles de Rais in me.

The visit was due for midday, but the noontide bell tolled, and the lunch hour came and went, and no car had pulled up at the gate and no joyous shouts of the Little Ones had been heard. The Colonel paced, wrist clasped in a hand behind him, or stationed himself before the window, muzzle thrust forward, and shot a cuff and lifted his arm to eye level and glared reproachfully at his watch. Miss Vavasour and I went about on tenterhooks, not daring to speak. The aroma of roasting chicken in the house seemed a heartless gibe. It was late in the afternoon when the telephone in the hall rang, making us all start. The Colonel leaned his ear to the receiver like a despairing priest in the confessional. The exchange was brief. We tried not to hear what he was saying. He came into the kitchen clearing his throat. 'Car,' he said, looking at no one. 'Broke down.' Clearly he had been lied to, or was lying now to us. He turned to Miss Vavasour with a desolate smile. 'Sorry about the chicken,' he said.

I encouraged him to come out for a drink with me but he declined. He was feeling a bit tired, he said, had a bit of a headache all of a sudden. He went off to his room. How heavy his tread was on the stair, how softly he closed the bedroom door. 'Oh, dear,' Miss Vavasour said.

I went to the Pier Head Bar by myself and got sozzled. I did not mean to but I did. It was one of those plangent autumn evenings streaked with late sunlight that seemed itself a memory of what sometime in the far past had been the blaze of noon. Rain earlier had left puddles on the road that were paler than the sky, as if the last of day were dying in them. It was windy and the skirts of my overcoat flapped about my legs like Little Ones of my own, begging their Da not to go to the pub. But go I did. The Pier Head is a cheerless establishment presided over by a huge television set, fully the match of Miss V.'s Panoramic, permanently switched on but with the sound turned down. The publican is a fat soft slow man of few words. He has a peculiar name, I cannot remember it for the moment. I drank double brandies. Odd moments of the evening stand out in my memory, fuzzily bright, like lamp standards in a fog. I remember provoking or being provoked into an argument with an old fellow at the bar, and being remonstrated with by a much younger one, his son, perhaps, or grandson, whom I pushed and who threatened to summon the police. When the publican intervened – Barragry, that is his name – I tried to push him, too, lunging at him across the counter with a hoarse shout. Really, this is not like me at all, I do not know what was the matter, I mean other than what is usually the matter. At last they calmed me down and I retreated grumpily to a table in the corner, under the speechless television set, where I sat mumbling to myself and sighing. Those drunken sighs, bubbly and tremulous, how like sobs they can sound. The last light of evening, what I could see of it through the unpainted top quarter of the pub window, was of that angry, purplish-brown cast that I find both affecting and troubling, it is the very colour of winter. Not that I have anything against winter, indeed, it is my favourite season, next to autumn, but this year that November glow seemed a presagement of something more than winter, and I fell into a mood of bitter melancholy. Seeking to assuage my heaviness of heart I called for more brandy but Barragry refused it, advisedly, as I now acknowledge, and I stormed out in rageful indignation, or tried to storm but staggered really, and came back to the Cedars and my own bottle, which I have fondly dubbed the Little Corporal. On the stairs I met Colonel Blunden and had some converse with him, I do not know what about, exactly.

It was night by now, but instead of staying in my room and going to bed I put the bottle under my coat and went out again. Of what happened after that I have only jagged and ill-lit flickers of recollection. I remember standing in the wind under the shaking radiance of a street light awaiting some grand and general revelation and then losing interest in it before it could arrive. Then I was on the beach in the dark, sitting in the sand with my legs stuck out before me and the brandy bottle, empty now or nearly, cradled in my lap. There seemed to be lights out at sea, a long way from shore, bobbing and swaying, like the lights of a fishing fleet, but I must have imagined them, there are no fishing boats in these waters. I was cold despite my coat, the thickness of which was not enough to protect my hindparts from the chill dampness of the sand in which I was sitting. It was not the damp and the chill, however, that made me struggle to my feet at last, but a determination to get closer to those lights and investigate them; I may even have had some idea of wading into the sea and swimming out to meet them. It was at the water's edge, anyway, that I lost my footing and fell down and struck my temple on a stone. I lay there for I do not know how long, fluttering in and out of consciousness, unable or unwilling to move. It is a good thing the tide was on the ebb. I was not in pain, not even very much upset. In fact, it seemed quite natural to be sprawled there, in the dark, under a tumultuous sky, watching the faint phosphorescence of the waves as they pattered forward eagerly only to retreat again, like a flock of inquisitive but timorous mice, and the Little Corporal, as drunk it seemed as myself, rolling back and forth on the shingle with a grating sound, and hearing the wind above me blowing through the great invisible hollows and funnels of the air.

I must have fallen asleep then, or passed out even, for I do not remember the Colonel finding me, although he insists I spoke to him quite sensibly, and allowed him to help me up and walk me back to the Cedars. This must have been the case, I mean I must have been in some way conscious, for he would not have had the strength, surely, to get me to my feet unassisted, much less to haul me from the beach to my bedroom door, slung across his back, perhaps, or dragging me by the heels behind him. But how had he known where to find me? It seems that in our colloquy on the stairs, although colloquy is not the word, since according to him I did the most part of the talking, I had dwelt at length on the well-known fact, well known and a fact according to me, that drowning is the gentlest death, and when by a late hour he had not heard me returning, and fearing that I might indeed in my inebriated state try to make away with myself, he had decided he must go and look for me. He had to scout the beach for a long time, and had been about to give up the search, when some gleam from moon or brightest star fell upon my form, supine there on that stony littoral. When, after much meandering and many pauses for expatiation by me on numerous topics, we arrived at the Cedars at last, he had helped me up the stairs and seen me into my room. All this reported, for of that faltering anabasis I recall, as I have said, nothing. Later he had heard me, still in my room, being uproariously sick – not on the carpet but out of the window into the back yard, I am relieved to say – and then seeming to fall down heavily, and had taken it upon himself to come into my room, and there had discovered me, for the second time that night, in a heap, as they say, at the foot of the bed, lost to consciousness and, so he judged, urgently in need of medical attention.

I woke at some early hour of the still-dark

morning to a strange and unnerving scene which I at first took to be an hallucination. The Colonel was there, spick as usual in tweed and cavalry twill – he had not been to bed at all – pacing the floor with a frown, and so, far more implausibly, was Miss Vavasour, who, it would turn out, also had heard, or felt, more likely, in the very bones of the old house, the crash I made as I collapsed after that bout of vomiting at the window. She was wearing her Japanese dressing-gown, and her hair was gathered under a hair-net the like of which I had not seen since I was a child. She sat on a chair a little way off from me, against the wall, sideways on, in the very pose of Whistler's mother, her hands folded on her lap and her face bowed, so that her eye sockets seemed two pits of empty blackness. A lamp, which I thought was a candle, was burning on a table before her, shedding a dim globe of light upon the scene, which overall – a dimly radiant round with seated woman and pacing man – might have been a nocturnal study by Géricault, or de la Tour. Baffled, and abandoning all effort to understand what was going on or how the two of them came to be there, I fell asleep again, or passed out again.

When I next awakened the curtains were open and it was day. The room had a chastened and somewhat abashed aspect, I thought, and everything looked pale and featureless, like a woman's unmade-up morning face. Outside, a uniformly white sky sat sulkily immobile, seeming no more than a yard or two higher than the roof of the house. Vaguely the events of the night came shuffling back shamefaced to my addled consciousness. Around me the bed-clothes were tossed and twisted as after a debauch, and there was a strong smell of sick. I put up a hand and a shot of pain went through my head when my fingers found the pulpy swelling on my temple where it had struck upon the stone. It was only then, with a start that made the bed creak, that I noticed the young man seated on my chair, leaning forward with his arms folded on my desk, reading a book lying open before him on my leather writing pad. He wore steel-framed spectacles and had a high, balding brow and sparse hair of no particular colour. His clothes were characterless too, although I had a general impression of jaded corduroys. Hearing me stir he lifted his eyes unhurriedly from the page and turned his head and looked at me, quite composed, and even smiled, though cheerlessly, and enquired as to how I was feeling. Nonplussed – that is the word, surely – I struggled up in the bed, which seemed to wobble under me as if the mattress were filled with some thick and viscous liquid, and gave him what was intended to be an imperiously interrogative stare. However, he continued calmly regarding me, quite unruffled. The Doctor, he said, making it sound as though there were only one in the world, had been to see me earlier, while I was out – *out*, that was how he put it, and I wondered wildly for a moment if I had been down to the beach again, without knowing it – and had said I seemed to be suffering from a concussion compounded by severe but temporary alcohol poisoning. Seemed? Seemed?

'Claire drove us down,' he said. 'She's sleeping now.'

Jerome! The chinless inamorato! Now I knew him. How had he wormed his way back into my daughter's favour? Had he been the only one she could think of to turn to, in the middle of the night, when the Colonel or Miss Vavasour, whichever of them it was, had called to tell her of the latest scrape her father had got himself into? If so, I thought, I shall be to blame, although I could not see exactly why. How I cursed myself, sprawled there on that Doge's daybed, crapulent and woozy and altogether lacking the strength to leap up and seize the presumptuous fellow by the scruff and throw him out a second time. But there was worse to come. When he went out to find if Claire had wakened yet, and she came back with him, drawn and red-rimmed and wearing a raincoat over her slip, she informed me straight away, with the air of one hastily drawing fire so as to be able all the better to deflect it, that they were engaged. For a moment, befuddled as I was, I did not know what she meant – engaged by whom, and as what? – a moment which, as it proved, was sufficient for my vanquishment. I have not managed to bring up the subject again, and every further moment that passes further consolidates her victory over me. This is how, in a twinkling, these things are won and lost. Read Maistre on warfare.

Nor did she stop there, but, flushed with that initial triumph, and seizing the advantage offered by my temporary infirmity, went on to direct, a figurative hand cocked on her hip, that I must pack up and leave the Cedars forthwith and let her take me home – home, she says! – where she will care for me, which care will include, I am given to understand, the withholding of all alcoholic stimulants, or soporifics, until such time as the Doctor, him again, declares me fit for something or other, life, I suppose. What am I to do? How am I to resist? She says it is time I got down seriously to work. 'He is finishing,' she informed her betrothed, not without a gloss of filial pride, 'a big book on Bonnard.' I had not the heart to tell her that my Big Book on Bonnard – it sounds like something one might shy coconuts at – has got no farther than half of a putative first chapter and a notebook filled with derivative and half-baked would-be aperçus. Well, it is no matter. There are other things I can do. I can go to Paris and paint. Or I might retire into a monastery, pass my days in quiet contemplation of the infinite, or write a great treatise there, a vulgate of the dead, I can see myself in my cell, long-bearded, with quill-pen and hat and docile lion, through a window beside me minuscule peasants in the distance making hay, and hovering above my brow the dove refulgent. Oh, yes, life is pregnant with possibilities.

I suppose I shall not be allowed to sell the house, either.

Miss Vavasour says she will miss me, but thinks I am doing *the right thing*. Leaving the Cedars is hardly of my doing, I tell her, I am being forced to it. She smiles at that. 'Oh, Max,' she says, 'I do not think you are a man to be forced into anything.' That gives me pause, not because of the tribute to my strength of will, but the fact, which I register with a faint shock, that this is the first time she has addressed me by my name. Still, I do not think it means that I can call her Rose. A certain formal distance is necessary for the good maintenance of the dainty relation we have forged, re-forged, between us over these past weeks. At this hint of intimacy, however, the old, unasked questions come swarming forward again. I would like to ask her if she blames herself for Chloe's death – I believe, I should say, on no evidence, that it was Chloe who went down first, with Myles following after, to try to save her – and if she is convinced their drowning together like that was entirely an accident, or something else. She would probably tell me, if I did ask. She is not reticent. She fairly prattled on about the Graces, Carlo and Connie – 'Their lives were destroyed, of course' – and how they, too, died, not long after losing the twins. Carlo went first, of an aneurysm, then Connie, in a car crash. I ask what kind of crash, and she gives me a look. 'Connie was not the kind to kill herself,' she says, with a faint twist of the lips.

They were good to her, afterwards, she says, never a reproach or the hint of an accusation of duty betrayed. They set her up at the Cedars, they knew Bun's people, persuaded them to take her on to look after the house. 'And here I am still,' she says, with a grim small smile, 'all these long years later.'

The Colonel is moving about upstairs, making

discreet but definite noises; he is glad I am going, I know it. I thanked him for his help last night. 'You probably saved my life,' I said, thinking suddenly it was probably true. Much huffing and clearing of the throat – *Faugh, sir, only doin' me demned duty!* – and a hand giving my upper arm a quick squeeze. He even produced a going-away present, a fountain pen, a Swan, it is as old as he is, I should think, still in its box, in a bed of yellowed tissue paper. I am graving these words with it, it has a graceful action, smooth and swift with only the occasional blot. Where did he come by it, I wonder? I did not know what to say. 'Nothing required,' he said. 'Never had a use for it myself, you should have it, for your writing, and so on.' Then he bustled off, rubbing his white old dry hands together. I note that although it is not the weekend he is wearing his yellow waistcoat. I shall never know, now, if he really is an old army man, or an impostor. It is another of those questions I cannot bring myself to put to Miss Vavasour.

'It's her I miss,' she says, 'Connie – Mrs Grace – that is.' I suppose I stare, and she gives me another of those pitying glances. 'It was never him, with me,' she says. 'You didn't think that, did you?' I thought of her standing below me that day under the trees, sobbing, her head sitting on the platter of her fore-

262

shortened shoulders, the wadded hankie in her hand. 'Oh, no,' she said, 'never him.' And I thought, too, of the day of the picnic and of her sitting behind me on the grass and looking where I was avidly looking and seeing what was not meant for me at all.

Anna died before dawn. To tell the truth, I was not there when it happened. I had walked out on to the steps of the nursing home to breathe deep the black and lustrous air of morning. And in that moment, so calm and drear, I recalled another moment, long ago, in the sea that summer at Ballyless. I had gone swimming alone, I do not know why, or where Chloe and Myles might have been; perhaps they had gone with their parents somewhere, it would have been one of the last trips they made together, perhaps the very last. The sky was hazed over and not a breeze stirred the surface of the sea, at the margin of which the small waves were breaking in a listless line, over and over, like a hem being turned endlessly by a sleepy seamstress. There were few people on the beach, and those few were at a distance from me, and something in the dense, unmoving air made the sound of their voices seem to come from a greater distance still. I was standing up to my waist in water that was perfectly transparent, so that I could plainly see below me the ribbed sand of the seabed, and tiny shells and bits of a crab's broken claw, and my own feet, pallid and alien, like specimens displayed under glass. As I stood there, suddenly, no, not suddenly, but in a sort of driving heave, the whole sea surged, it was not a wave, but a smooth rolling swell that seemed to come up from the deeps, as if something vast down there had stirred itself, and I was lifted briefly and carried a little way towards the shore and then was set down on my feet as before, as if nothing had happened. And indeed nothing had happened, a momentous nothing, just another of the great world's shrugs of indifference.

A nurse came out then to fetch me, and I turned and followed her inside, and it was as if I were walking into the sea.